PRAISE FOR
Don't I Know You?

"[T]he most suspenseful and moving novel I've read in many years. . . . This is a book that haunts and tantalizes and possesses us long after the last page is turned."

—Tim O'Brien, author of *The Things They Carried*

"Riveting and deeply felt and true."   —Dave Eggers, author of *A Heartbreaking Work of Staggering Genius*

"I generally feel skeptical when someone says they've read a book in one sitting. Don't you ever get thirsty, answer the phone, or want to check on the basketball scores? But *Don't I Know You?* truly is one of those books you tear through at a tremendous clip, driven, I believe, by the anxiety-ridden delusion that if you can get to the end in time you can save Karen Shepard's delicately drawn characters from their fates. Shepard's gritty, sympathetic evocation of the pre-boom Upper West Side and a handful of its haunted inhabitants is as logical and troubling as a dream, and even when its central mystery is more or less solved, the larger mysteries it evokes remain chillingly intact."   —Scott Spencer, National Book Award finalist for *A Ship Made of Paper*

"In spare, elliptical, dispassionate prose, Karen Shepard drops the stone of murder into a pond and watches as the widening ripples affect even those far removed from the victim. *Don't I Know You?* is a chilly, disquieting mystery in which the answer is always 'no.'"   —Ron Hansen, author of *Mariette in Ecstasy* and the National Book Award finalist *Atticus*

"[An] intriguing mystery in four parts . . . the reader is led to sort through disparate strands to discover the connections and to wonder what happened and why . . . making for a nicely paced story."　　　　　　　　　　　　　　—*Library Journal*

"[In this] masterful third book . . . Shepard's narrative unravels Gina's murder obliquely, through her characters' layered relationships, leading to a conclusion that's satisfying, haunting, and well deserved."　　　　　　　—*Publishers Weekly* (starred review)

"Karen Shepard's *Don't I Know You?* unravels the mystery of a single mother's death obliquely, through the poignant gaze of the victim's twelve-year-old son and the layered relationships of unnervingly familiar characters."　　　　　　　　—*Vogue*

"*Don't I Know You?* is both a literary novel and a mystery, but its mystery is less who committed the grisly crime on which it centers than the mysteries of human psychology. . . . [It has] precise, perfectly pitched prose and deep psychological insights. . . . And although each of the characters in this complex book comes fully alive, the reader is left with more questions than answers, a powerful reminder of the ways in which our knowledge is always limited."　　　　　　　—*Houston Chronicle*

"*Don't I Know You?* is a brilliantly understated and hauntingly evocative whodunit powered by characterization, an addictively intimate narrative, and an ultra-complex plot that will have readers guessing until the very last pages. . . . Easily one of the most intriguing mystery/thrillers of the year."

—Barnes & Noble.com

"Shepard carries out this fascinating premise with exquisite skill, offering a trio of distinctive voices, doubting perspectives, and the small acts that build to momentous consequence."

—*New Orleans Times-Picayune*

"[This] cunningly crafted jigsaw puzzle is colored by vibrant prose and capped by a you'll-never-guess conclusion that's not the least bit gimmicky. You might want to read it all over again."

—*Entertainment Weekly*

"Shepard has found a voice here that is strong and confident and full of wise observation." —*O, The Oprah Magazine*

"The author of this extraordinary whodunit does know you: She knows how a heart has misgivings. She also knows New York in the 1970s in every gritty detail. And she knows how to tell a good story. We read it in one standing." —*More* magazine

"Karen Shepard's gripping whodunit . . . has a unique format: The story unfolds through the distinct perspectives of three characters, reminding you that reality is in the eye of the beholder." —*Marie Claire*

"The suspense only grows as the rippling effects of the murder are closely observed. Meanwhile, Shepard is almost offhanded in giving up the actual killer, thereby ensuring that the disclosure has stunning impact. *Don't I Know You?* is both subtle and disturbing in just the right proportions." —*New York Daily News*

"*Don't I Know You?* will no doubt be marketed as a hybrid form, a literary thriller or literary mystery or literary suspense novel, but in fact it adheres much more strenuously to straight-up literary realism. This is the way we live now: never knowing for sure the contents of another's heart. Shepard's haunting novel proposes the alluring mystery of a particular murder and its specific repercussions, but in doing so she also summons the larger mystery of human character, the multiple and complex circuitry that knits together the community in which unsolved violence occurs. The book is an insightful psychological thriller, but it's also thrilling psychological insight."

—Antonya Nelson, author of
Talking in Bed and *Female Trouble: Stories*

Barry Goldstein

About the Author

KAREN SHEPARD is a Chinese American born and raised in New York City. She is the author of the novels *An Empire of Women* and *The Bad Boy's Wife*. Her work has appeared in *The Atlantic Monthly*, *Self*, and *Bomb*, among other publications. She teaches writing and literature at Williams College in Williamstown, Massachusetts, where she lives with her husband, writer Jim Shepard, and their three children.

don't
i know
you?

KAREN SHEPARD

HARPER ⬤ PERENNIAL

NEW YORK ● LONDON ● TORONTO ● SYDNEY

For Steven

HARPER ❖ PERENNIAL

A hardcover edition of this book was published in 2006 by
Willam Morrow, an imprint of HarperCollins Publishers.

HarperCollins books may be purchased for educational, business,
or sales promotional use. For information please write:
Special Markets Department, HarperCollins Publishers,
10 East 53rd Street, New York, NY 10022.

FIRST HARPER PERENNIAL EDITION PUBLISHED 2007.

Designed by Claire Vaccaro

The Library of Congress has catalogued the hardcover
edition as follows:

Shepard, Karen.
    Don't I know you? : a novel / Karen Shepard.—1st ed.
        p. cm.
    ISBN: 978-0-06-078237-5 (acid-free paper)
    ISBN-10: 0-06-078237-4 (acid-free paper)
        1. Manhattan (New York N.Y.)—Fiction.   I. Title.

PS3569.H39388D66 2006
813'.6—dc22
                                                        2005056254

ISBN: 978-0-06-078238-2 (pbk.)
ISBN-10: 0-06-078238-2 (pbk.)

07 08 09 10 11 ❖/RRD 10 9 8 7 6 5 4 3 2 1

I

August 1976

one

It was just a Tuesday. Steven's key worked like it always had.

His mother was lying between the living room and the front hall. He saw her feet first. They were bare, and at first he thought she was doing her yoga.

She was on her side. Her bottom leg was straight. Her top one was bent. One arm was stretched above her. Her head was resting on it. Her other arm was bent across her middle. Her hand was in a fist.

Her dress was up around her waist. Her panties were ripped. He could see her blue birthmark below her belly button. There were scratches on her thighs. There was a lot of blood.

The green rug from the hall was bunched underneath her hip and bloody. The phone was on its side next to her. It was bloody.

The windows were open. Down there on the corner of 102nd and West End, Ramon and Jimmy were sitting on their over- turned crates drinking beer, smoking, trying to stay cool. He could hear them. The fans were on. She smelled wrong. The TV was on. The sound was off.

He stood there. He'd been up high on a catwalk for the spring musical. It felt like that now.

His body was shaking as if he were freezing, but sweat beaded under his bangs and between his shoulder blades.

Kitty came from somewhere down the hall and circled his legs. He tried to pet her, but couldn't stop the trembling.

Manuel's voice came up through the windows. "Not in a minute," he was saying. "Now. Before now. Yesterday."

He walked by her, closing his eyes, to the TV. A nature show. He turned it off and watched the screen until the dot in the center disappeared. The shaking was going away. He was still cold. They'd had this TV for a hundred years. When Starsky and Hutch walked toward him they looked like people in a dream. Yesterday, he'd been after her about getting a better one.

Hot air blew around him from outside. He felt like the guy on *Wild Kingdom* getting licked by cheetah cubs.

He sat cross-legged across the room from her for a minute. Kitty leaned against his knee, making her small engine sounds deep in her throat.

He couldn't tell where she'd been stabbed. He was sleepy.

He'd spent the day in the park, climbing rocks and breaking sticks with Juan. They'd eaten peanut-butter-and-honey sandwiches and shared a Yoo-hoo. There'd been a dead pigeon in the sandbox. "Don't touch it," Juan had said. "You'll get rabbis."

His mother was Greek; sometimes she got words wrong.

They'd poked at it with a stick, and then they'd washed their hands anyway, proud of their good thinking. He had used the water fountain. Juan had used the puddle around the sprinklers.

He wasn't thinking the things he was supposed to be thinking.

He'd only been home for a few minutes. He asked himself what he was feeling. None of this was happening.

Outside, it was getting darker. Inside too. He was crying.

Her black hair was still in its ponytail. It was spread out like she was jumping. She was making a face that he didn't like to look at. He thought about touching her, but didn't.

Down the hall, a quiet thud and two creaks.

His feet and hands tingled. *Get out,* he thought. He stood; his knees cracked, and he headed toward the front door. The sound of something heavy being lifted and put down again. He was still crying. He started down the hall. He couldn't believe he was doing it.

There was blood. Streaky patches of it. And then it stopped. His foot hit something that rolled. Glass beads. He recognized them from the necklace she liked to wear.

Her bedroom door was open a little. Shadows moved behind it.

He ran the last few feet. His head felt like he'd been holding his breath too long. "Hey," he called. "Hey."

One leg was disappearing out the window onto the fire escape. Jeans. A white sock. Adidas sneaker. White with green stripes.

The room was a mess, but there was no blood.

"Hey," he said again. "You," he called, hating himself for being stupid and twelve and sounding like a girl.

He stuck his head out as far as he could. His mother didn't like him to. He saw someone running. A man in a white T-shirt. It was too dark to see anything else. He couldn't even tell what color hair the guy had.

The bed looked like someone had made it and then run back and forth across it. Everything else looked the same.

He felt like he was looking at things through a ViewMaster. His stomach was cramping. His head felt cut in half.

He went and stood in her closet. When he was little, he would sneak in there in the middle of the night. He would sit on the floor on top of her shoes and handbags and dirty clothes. He was supposed to be able to spend the whole night in his own room. His doctor had told her that. If she had to, he'd told her, she could always put a latch on the outside of the boy's bedroom door. "What's the worst that could happen?" he'd said. "He'll fall asleep crying by the door."

She never did. So he'd fall asleep in her closet, and she'd find him in the morning. One night he opened the door and there was a sleeping bag and pillow. The sleeping bag was unzipped partway and turned down. After that, he didn't go in there anymore.

The closet smelled like dust and blankets and sweaters and her. Sometimes when she'd had a long day, she'd stay in the shower, standing under the hot water for way longer than it took to get clean. She said that on days like those it was just the best place to be. Under the water, by herself.

The doorbell rang. Kitty meowed. Sometimes she thought she was a dog. It was what his mom liked about her.

The clock on her dresser said 8:48. It was almost dark out. The doorbell rang again. He was supposed to have watched the nature shows with her that night. They usually did, but he'd been having fun with Juan.

He stood there, breathing the way he did at the top of the skateboard ramp in the park. If it was late enough in the day for the sun to be behind you, you were flying and you were invisible. Get ready, he thought on days like that. Get ready to disappear.

He almost expected to hear her answer the door. Not really, but it wouldn't have totally surprised him.

The bell rang a few more times, and then he heard a key in the lock. He sat under his mother's clothes. She liked batik and hats with wide, sagging brims. The Puerto Rican guys on the block said she had style. But the moms at his school wore better clothes, had better hair, did their makeup differently. She didn't look like the moms at school. She looked like those mothers from the ABC After School Specials. A little worn out. Someone who never got a break.

He pulled some shoes around him like a moat. It helped a little, being in here. Until he was six, and kids at school started teasing him, she used to paint his nails.

Someone made an animal sound. Someone called his name. Phil, the boyfriend. He thought he'd answered, but Phil wasn't acting like he'd heard anything. He was calling it louder as he got closer, in a voice that didn't sound like his. Phil found him on the floor of her closet, holding her sun hat in his lap. Like a baby. Like someone who didn't know anything about anything.

He crawled in there with him. His skin was blotchy. "Hey there," he said. He sounded like he was working to keep his voice from doing things. And then he didn't say anything else. He was trying to keep his body still. His eyes were moving all over the place. He was red, like he was embarrassed.

He didn't have anything against Phil.

Two years ago, Phil had been his fifth-grade teacher. Steven had spent the year forgetting homework, losing lunch boxes, messing up on tests. At the spring parent conference, Phil had looked across the Formica table at Steven's mother and had done nothing but talk about what an addition to the class Steven was. He had artistic gifts. A real theatrical streak. Beyond-his-years perceptive abilities. He was funny, but always in appropriate ways. Nothing about that disengaged aloofness grown-ups often tried to talk him out of. Nothing about the stuff Steven had been caught writing in the boys' bathroom. Nothing about picking at the skin around his thumbnails or pulling his eyebrows out. That's when Steven knew, and his mother knew he knew. Under the table, she'd reached over and squeezed his knee.

A few months ago, she'd asked what he'd think about her and Phil getting married, them moving to a new place.

"Like a new apartment?" he'd said, kind of excited about the possibilities. He'd seen where some of the other kids at school lived, the ones who weren't scholarship kids. Neighborhoods without transistor radios in open windows, old ladies with head-scarves behind them. No abandoned buildings with murals of the Puerto Rican flag.

"Well, yes," she'd said in that careful way that made him know she was worried. "But also a new place place. Like a new town."

"Town?" he'd said. He liked City. He didn't think he was really Town material.

"Don't worry about it," she'd said. "Nothing's gonna happen for a while." She hadn't talked about it since then, and he hadn't wanted to remind her, though a few weeks after they'd talked, the three of them had gone hiking. They'd taken the train to Cold Spring Harbor, walked from the train station to a state park, con-sulted Phil's map, and made their way up a steep trail a couple of miles long to a rocky outcropping at the top of a small mountain. Steven had been in charge of pointing out trail markers, quick yellow brushstrokes, arm height on the sides of trees. They'd come across a mound of sticks and logs that looked like a home for giant beavers, and his mother had let him climb it. At the top of the mountain, they'd sat on the warm rocks and eaten hard-boiled eggs and boiled potatoes with salt, Phil's Famous Granola, and apricots. A pair of hang gliders had appeared and drifted in front of them, close enough to see their smiles. Steven had waved, and one of them had said, "Later," before sweeping out of range.

"I guess we'd better call the police," Phil said quietly. It sounded like there was something big in his throat. Steven tried to imagine what looking at a dead girlfriend would feel like.

He felt like cooled lava. If he opened his mouth things would crack apart.

"Do you want to stay in here?" Phil asked.

Steven nodded.

He stood. "You gonna be okay?" he asked.

Steven didn't know whether he meant in the closet or something bigger. He shrugged.

Phil said he'd be right in the bedroom, and he left the closet door open.

While he was on the phone, Steven crawled out quietly. He stayed on all fours all the way down the hall. He avoided the glass beads. He avoided the blood. Kitty thought it was a game. She batted at his face. He hissed.

Phil had turned on the front hall light. Now Steven turned it off. The streetlights made everything look orange.

He imagined her as modeling clay. As the wet sand at Jones Beach the day they'd made handprints at the edge of the ocean.

What he was doing now was like that, only slower.

. . . .

the guys in uniforms arrived first. Policemen and ambulance guys. One of the officers had Phil take him around the apartment. Phil kept saying, "I told you. There's nothing missing." Another guy had Steven do the same thing. The policeman turned on all the lights as they walked around.

The ambulance guys bent over her for a while. They had lots of equipment that they didn't use. Steven watched them from the couch. One looked up at another and said, "DOA." The other asked where the 124 man was. They didn't seem all that interested in him. One of them threw fresh coffee grounds into a small frying pan and turned on the stove. The smell filled the room. There was a tall guy everyone called Dutch.

Phil finished with the policeman and came and sat next to Steven on the couch. He put his hand on Steven's leg and rocked it back and forth. He reached up and turned off the lamp at the end of the couch.

Steven checked his watch. It was almost midnight, and the apartment still felt like the inside of the Laundromat. It smelled like coffee and his mother. It was hard to keep his eyes open.

More guys arrived. The Photo and Fingerprint Unit. The photo deputy took photos of her. Straight down and sideways. Another guy circled each one of the glass beads with chalk. Someone else put paper bags over her hands. Steven didn't ask what for.

Two detectives arrived. McGuire and Adams. A uniform guy said, "No weapon," then nodded in Steven's direction. "There's the boy."

They offered their condolences. Adams looked a little better dressed. He said he was from Homicide; McGuire was from the local squad. McGuire caught Steven's eye and rolled his eyes a little. Steven didn't know what he meant.

"First things first," McGuire said. "Let's get these uniforms outta here. They're like visiting relatives; all they do is stomp around messing up the place."

Phil and Steven sat there.

Detective Adams asked if there was a neighbor's apartment they could set up shop in. They needed to secure the scene. The Medical Examiner was on his way.

Phil looked at Steven. Steven tried to imagine ringing the Gonzalezes' doorbell, or the Rifkins'.

"There's Manuel," Phil said. "He's the super. He's got an apartment on the first floor."

Detective McGuire nodded. He seemed to be making a little sketch of the area in his notebook.

The Medical Examiner arrived. He was a big man with an unlit cigar in his mouth. He bent over the body. Detective Adams knelt next to him and put on rubber gloves. They talked in low voices for a few minutes. Steven heard, ". . . haphazard *and* fastidious."

A guy working on fingerprints complained about how dirty everything was. He wasn't going to get anything here, he said.

Detective Adams found something under her fist. He held it up for Steven. It was a silver bracelet with an infinity sign on it. "Was this hers?" he asked.

Steven nodded. She had a lot of bracelets.

Detective Adams handed it up to a uniform guy, then stood slowly, his hands pushing on his knees. Steven watched them.

The Medical Examiner cut a piece of her hair. He took off the paper bags, trimmed her fingernails, and put everything into small envelopes. He glanced at Steven, then said something to Adams. "Get it later," Adams said, also looking at Steven. Steven didn't care what they were talking about.

The Medical Examiner knelt on one knee and put a manila tag on the body's big toe.

When they lifted her into the bag, her hair moved like it always had. Some of it got caught in the zipper. The guy had to yank at it a couple of times. The plastic made a heavy sound, like clapping underwater. When he saw Steven watching him, the guy blushed and shrugged.

They put her on the stretcher and started wheeling her out. Steven stood and followed them to the entryway. Phil followed. Steven curled his toes inside his sneakers until they hurt.

Manuel was in the hallway. He gave a wave. Steven wanted to wave back, but his hands wouldn't work.

"That's Manuel," Phil said to Detective Adams.

Detective Adams went to talk with Manuel. Steven watched. He watched the elevator arrive. He watched the ambulance guys push her in.

"Where do they take her?" he asked anyone who was listening.

"To the city morgue," Detective McGuire said. "At Bellevue."

Juan lived near there. They'd biked by it the other day.

Detective Adams gestured to Detective McGuire.

McGuire put his hand on Steven's shoulder. "Can you do me a favor?" he asked.

Steven shrugged.

"Do you have a couple of photos of your mom? Snapshots. Anything."

"On the corkboard in the kitchen," he said. "What for?" he added.

McGuire headed into the kitchen. "For the files and for interviewing people in the neighborhood," he said.

It seemed like a straightforward answer.

McGuire came back out of the kitchen.

"Which ones did you take?" Steven asked.

McGuire showed him. One from the beach last summer. Another that Phil had taken on the roof just a couple of weeks ago. "Those are good," Steven said.

"Why don't you and me head downstairs," McGuire said. "Get you something to eat or something."

Steven shrugged and looked around. "Should I bring anything?" he asked.

McGuire waved a thick hand. "Nah," he said. "You can get what you need later."

Phil started out with them. McGuire put a hand on his arm. "Detective Adams will be taking you down in a minute; if you could just wait for him here," he said. He called a uniform guy over and told Phil that the officer would look out for him until Detective Adams got back.

"I don't need looking after," Phil said.

Detective McGuire put his hands up. "Didn't mean nothing by it," he said.

"I want to be with Steven," Phil said.

Detective McGuire shook his head. "Not right now, sir. Not right now." He nodded at the officer, who held Phil's elbow and steered him to the couch. It was gentle, like he was taking him out onto the dance floor.

Phil looked at Steven over his shoulder. "I'll be right up here," he said. "If you need anything, you make them come get me."

Steven nodded.

"I'm not hungry," he said.

"Thirsty?" Detective McGuire asked.

Steven shook his head.

"Well, I'm thirsty," McGuire said. "This heat, I'm drinking my weight in Cokes." He patted his belly.

He looked like a detective. He had on worn black dress shoes, a sport jacket, a tie frayed at the edges. They looked like clothes someone else had picked out for him from four different closets.

On their way out of the apartment, Steven reached into the basket on the table by the door and slipped his mother's keys into his pocket. He held his hand around them so they wouldn't make any noise.

Detective McGuire pressed the down button. The elevator made its sounds. Someone was making stir-fry.

"I love Chinese," Detective McGuire said. "You?"

They used to go to Moon Palace after school on Wednesdays for dumplings and shredded pork with Peking sauce. His mother was nice to the owner, so Steven got free Shirley Temples.

"Your mom cook Chinese?" McGuire asked.

It felt like no one had talked about her until right then.

Steven shook his head. "She was Italian," he said. "Mostly Italian," he added. "Some German." He didn't know why he was telling him this stuff.

"Mostly Italians like Chinese," he said.

Steven didn't argue.

"You ever go down to Chinatown for dim sum?" he asked.

He had, once. A place with the steepest, longest escalator he'd ever been on. He nodded. "Some place with an escalator," he said. "Near the Manhattan Bridge." They'd been with a friend of his mother's. A big Russian guy. When they went to restaurants, it was always with a guy.

McGuire nodded. "I been there. That's a good place."

They watched the numbers. Half of them didn't light up anymore.

"Amazing," McGuire said. "Amazing how they can get all that stuff into those little dumplings." He really seemed amazed.

Steven's insides felt like he had a fever, but when he touched his cheek, his skin was cool. It was like he was touching someone else's head. He leaned his forehead against the wall of the elevator. He could feel its hum through his skull.

"Okay?" Detective McGuire asked.

Steven closed his eyes and shook his head.

"You're in a kind of shock," McGuire said. He put his hand on Steven's forehead under his bangs like he was checking for a fever and left it there for the rest of the ride. A few years ago, he'd had a fever of 105. His mother and the boyfriend who'd taught him to ride a bike had soaked washcloths in alcohol and tucked them under his arms.

Manuel, his wife, Tina, and their two little girls were standing in a group outside their apartment staring. Tina ran to hug him. Her apron smelled of plantains and felt rough and worn, like the punching bag Michael from upstairs used to have. He let her hug him as long as she wanted.

Detective McGuire tugged his T-shirt gently. "Come on in," he said.

"You tell them everything," Tina said. "You tell them everything you know so they can catch this guy and let him rot in jail."

"Tina," Manuel said softly, touching her arm.

Manuel thought she was hotheaded. She thought he was too nice. Too good for his own good, she told Steven's mother. His mother said their arguing was a sign of how much they loved each other.

their apartment had the same layout. They crowded into the kitchen. Detective Adams was on the phone. He sounded like he was talking to his boss. Steven wondered what Phil was doing upstairs.

Detective McGuire poured himself a glass of water. There was coffee in the coffee pot and a full mug on the counter. The mug was blue and orange. Manuel liked the Mets. Tina liked them more. Manuel and Tina shared a coffee every night after the girls went to bed. Sometimes, if his mother was out, Steven hung out down here with them. He figured they'd had to wake the girls up. He felt bad about that. He wondered where they were waiting while their kitchen was being used.

Detective Adams got off the phone and looked at him. "How you doing?" he asked.

"Okay," Steven said.

"It'll get better," he said. "I know it doesn't seem like it now, but it will."

He might've been right; he might've been wrong. Steven had no idea. It was a nice thing to say. People being nice to him always made his molars ache.

Adams told Detective McGuire he'd go get Phil and that they'd use the living room. Detective McGuire said they'd stay in here.

Adams left and McGuire sat at the table next to Steven. He pulled a bag of mini Goldenberg Peanut Chews from his jacket pocket and offered it to him. Steven took one and unwrapped it and held it in his hand looking at it. McGuire popped two into his mouth at once.

"How 'bout we talk a little," he said. It wasn't a question.

"Okay," he said.

He could see the detective's notebook in his shirt pocket. He left it there.

"Okay." He pushed his chair back and leaned forward on his thighs. "I know this is gonna be hard, and I'm sorry we have to do any of this, but whatever you can tell us will help us catch whoever did this. And that's what we all want."

Steven hadn't been thinking about the guy at all. What was wrong with him?

"Start at the beginning," McGuire said. He put the bag of peanut chews on the table. "Try not to leave anything out."

He left out the part about the closet. He left out the touching her part. He left out feeling like a baby.

When he got to the part about the guy in the bedroom, McGuire raised his eyebrows, and then he said, "Sometimes in situations like these you don't think; you just do."

I'm a situation, Steven thought.

"Did you recognize the guy?" McGuire asked.

"Everyone has those sneakers," Steven said.

McGuire smiled. "Tell me about your mom," he said.

The second he said it, Steven didn't have a thing to say.

He wasn't being a wise guy. It felt like whatever he said next was it. It would be who she was, the way they all remembered her.

If she wore her hair in a ponytail for too long, she got a headache. Her feet were always sore. Sometimes she switched price tags on things they couldn't afford. She said her waist was tiny, her hips were wide, and all her pants gapped around the waist. She rolled her socks around her hand before putting them in her sock drawer. She had vaccination marks on both her arms. She played the Who when she was sad. She wore her mother's wedding ring on her pinky. She had brown eyes and thick black eyebrows that she never plucked. She wore lipstick called Pink Chocolate. When she smiled, she looked like somebody famous.

He didn't say any of that. The peanut chew was melted. He closed his hand around it.

"How 'bout your dad?" Detective McGuire asked. "Is he around?"

"San Diego," Steven said. "They're divorced. Since I was six months old."

"Does he visit?" he asked.

Steven shook his head. "Not me," he said.

Detective McGuire uncurled Steven's fingers and took the melted candy. He took a handkerchief out of his pants pocket and wiped Steven's hand.

"I'm divorced," he said. "I got two kids; two girls. Every Wednesday night for dinner; every other weekend." He sounded like he was reciting a poem.

"If I was your dad—" he said. He looked at Steven sadly.

Steven waited for him to finish.

"Why'd they split?" McGuire asked.

Steven shrugged. "No one tells me anything," he said.

"D'your mom talk about him much?"

"Not really," Steven said.

"Did he help out with the bills?" McGuire asked.

"He pays for some of school," Steven said. For no reason, he added, "I got a scholarship for the rest."

Detective McGuire seemed unimpressed; he was folding his handkerchief into quarters.

"Must've been hard for your mom," he said. "On her own in the city; raising a kid."

"I guess," Steven said. "Are you gonna call my dad?" he asked.

"Yeah," McGuire said. "We'll call."

"I don't want to live with him," Steven said.

A few times, he'd looked up the number and called, daring himself to let it ring one more time before hanging up. Once, a man had answered, and Steven had frozen. "Hello? Hello?" the man had said before hanging up.

"Why not?" Detective McGuire asked.

Steven shrugged.

"It must've been nice," McGuire said. "Just you and your mom. That's something you could get used to."

She liked white rice with melted cheddar on top. She ate and drank things Steven wouldn't touch: millet, Postum, sprouts. Never eat French onion soup on a first date, she'd told him. French onion soup, lobster, cherry tomatoes, big pieces of lettuce. Guys dumped her more often than she dumped them. Sometimes, over a couple of years, they dumped her more than once. At the Bicentennial fireworks last month, she'd covered her eyes instead of her ears. She was tired a lot.

It sounded like there was a party going on in the lobby. Detective Adams poked his head in the kitchen. "Must be thirty or forty people out there," he said. "Gave a statement to the reporters." He held up Steven's mother's address book. "Called the father," he said. "He's coming in tomorrow. Plastic surgeon." He left.

Detective McGuire gestured toward the living room with his head. "How long's she been with him?" he asked.

"A couple of years," Steven said.

"Huh," he said.

"What?" Steven said.

He spun a peanut chew around on the table. "Nothing," he said. "It's just surprising they hadn't moved in together. Two years. That's a long time." He leaned back and stretched his legs out, crossing them at the ankles. "She must've wanted to get remarried. Give you a real family."

"Me and her are a real family," Steven said.

"Sure, sure," he said. "But I don't know, there was something about Phil——" He ran his hand through his hair and shook his head like a horse. "Nah, I don't know. Like he was the kind of kid who wouldn't bring enough to share, you know what I mean?"

Steven didn't, but he nodded anyway. He remembered that he and his mom didn't matter much to McGuire.

"Who were her friends at work?" McGuire asked.

"She didn't really have friends," Steven said. "Christine. Angela." He tapered off.

"What do you think of Phil?" McGuire asked.

"He's good," Steven said. He wanted someone to tell him where he was going to sleep, and to take him there.

"Was she seeing anyone besides him?"

Steven shook his head.

"He seemed kinda angry to me," McGuire said. "He ever lose his temper?"

One time he'd thrown Steven's books off his shelf. Steven had done some drawings on what turned out to be important papers. Phil had called him a little shit. He'd apologized after.

"Not really," Steven said.

"What about with your mom?" McGuire asked. "It might've been why they hadn't moved in together. She might've been thinking of you," he said.

Once, a woman had shown up at the door when Phil wasn't there. Steven's mother was in the bedroom. He went to the door and looked through the peephole. The woman was pounding on the door, screaming for Phil. She had blond hair and a scarf around her neck and her coat was unbuttoned. She was screaming for him to come out, to talk to her. She was calling him a lot of things. Steven's mother came out of the bedroom, fastening her robe as she walked. She took Steven by the shoulders and pulled him away from the door, and they both stood there in the front hall, watching the door and listening to the woman on the other side of it.

"I don't know," Steven said. "I know what you're thinking," he said. "I'm not stupid."

"Of course you're not," McGuire said. "That's why I'm talking to you like this, because I know you're smart and you loved your mom and you want to help us catch who did this to her."

Phil and Detective Adams were talking in the other room. Every now and then he could make out something they were saying. "I don't think so." "Not that I know of." "No." "She didn't go to bars." "Yes." "No."

McGuire leaned forward and put his hands on the table. They were big and soft-looking. "I'll be honest with you, Steven. There was no sign of forced entry. Stabbings indicate more anger than guns. We got six stab wounds here. In cases like this, it's almost always someone she knew, and someone she knew pretty well."

He had a kind of pained expression, like he was embarrassed to be talking about it. Steven felt like he was hearing what he already knew.

"Sometimes it's about money. Sometimes it's about jealousy or love. Sometimes, if there's a kid, it's about custody." McGuire looked up. "That's why I was asking about your dad," he said.

"My dad didn't want me," Steven said. "They didn't fight about money."

McGuire shook his head slowly. He was like a bear doing a trick. "Dads," he said. "Sometimes they don't know what they want."

Outside, people coming home from the bars. There was laughter. Something hit a garbage can. Steven felt bad for wanting to go to bed so much.

"You're sure that bracelet was hers?"

"She had a lot of bracelets," Steven said.

McGuire nodded. "Did she drink?" he asked.

"Sometimes," Steven said.

"What did she like to drink?" McGuire asked.

"I don't know," Steven said. "Kahlua. Sometimes she let me make Kahlua milk shakes."

McGuire smiled and pulled out his notebook.

Sometimes she gave herself B-12 shots for the hangovers. It was okay, she always told Steven. She was a nurse.

It sounded like someone was walking around in the living room. He closed his eyes and tried to remember better the sounds the guy had made in her bedroom.

"We were gonna move in with Phil," Steven said.

"Oh?" McGuire said. "So I guess I was wrong." He smiled. "Sometimes I am. Not often, but sometimes."

"In a different town," Steven said. Someone she knew, he thought. He thought of all the people they knew. He imagined someone doing that to her.

"You okay?" Detective McGuire said. "Getting tired?"

"We were gonna live in a town," Steven said.

"Sounds good," McGuire said.

Someone she knew had done that to her. The guy he'd seen was someone she knew.

"We were all really happy about it," Steven said.

McGuire nodded. "You should be," he said.

Detective Adams came in. "You about all done?" he asked.

McGuire stood up. He held the edge of the table like he was thinking about lifting it.

"Where's Phil?" Steven said.

"I told him to go home; get some rest," Adams said. "We all need some rest. He said he'd call you in the morning."

"Where do I go?" Steven asked.

Adams checked his notebook. "Christine Mahoney?"

Christine from the hospital. Another nurse. His mother always listed her under Person to Contact in the Case of an Emergency.

"She's on her way," Adams said.

"C'mon," McGuire said, "we can wait out on the stoop. Get some air."

The lobby was empty. There was no one on the street. Steven had no idea what time it was. It was still warm, but cooler than in the apartment. Detective Adams said he'd see McGuire back at the precinct. He told Steven he had his condolences. He gave him his card.

Steven and McGuire sat on the bottom step, their knees up high.

When he walked with his mother, she would sometimes put her fingertips on the edge of his hood or the back of his collar. After a while, he knew to look ahead, knowing there'd be something she'd seen, something she was watching out for.

"What next?" Steven said.

McGuire rubbed his eyes with the heel of his hand. "You'll have to go ID the body," he said. "Someone can go with you."

Steven looked at the toes of his sneakers. The rubber was wearing away. He could see his socks.

"How will you find out what you need to find out?" he asked.

"There'll be an autopsy; that'll help," McGuire said.

Steven waited.

"We'll talk to her friends, to the neighbors."

Steven must've looked skeptical. McGuire said he'd rather canvas this kind of neighborhood than the East Side any day. "People hang out windows all day here," he said.

He was right.

"They might not tell us anything right away," he said. "Maybe they want to talk to a friend before they say anything. Maybe they just need a little prodding, a little encouragement." He said it took patience. He rubbed his hands like he was putting lotion on them.

"We'll find out the restaurants she liked, the grocery stores she used. We'll figure out what her day was like today. We'll talk to your father."

Steven was looking at his sneakers.

"You can help with things like that," McGuire said. "You can make a big difference."

The gay guys across the street were coming home arm in arm. They waved like they saw him sitting on the stoop every night at this hour. He waved back. "When you find out what her day was like will you tell me?" he asked.

"Sure," McGuire said. "Absolutely."

Steven scanned the street from West End to Riverside. There were still puddles in the gutter. Two days ago kids had cooled off in the hydrant Ramon had opened up.

Christine got out of a cab on the corner.

They stood, and McGuire held out his hand like Steven was a grown-up he'd met at a party. "I'll be in touch," he said.

"She liked that bar up by Columbia," Steven said. "I can't remember the name. She liked the college kids," he said.

McGuire looked at him and nodded. "Okay," he said. He gave Steven his card. "You call if you need anything. Or just want to talk."

"I don't miss her yet," Steven said.

McGuire held the back of Steven's neck with his big hand. "You will," he said.

Christine came up and held Steven's face. He felt like he'd spent the whole night being passed from hand to hand.

McGuire introduced himself and gave her another card.

"Her name was Regina," Steven told him. "Regina Teresa Fischetti Engel. But everyone called her Gina." McGuire knew all of this already, but Steven told him anyway.

One fall two years ago, between nursing jobs, she'd worked a temp job at *Natural History* magazine at the Museum of Natural History. Her office was behind two black doors at the end of the Mayan Gold exhibit. Something in the room made Steven's ears ring. They'd been invited to the employee Christmas party. Every year the museum decorated a giant tree with origami animals made by employees and their children. He and his mother sat at a folding table following the instructions of a college-age Japanese girl. He made two swans and a crane. His mother made a frog and a big cat.

Afterward, the children took turns finding spots for the animals on the tree. They let the bigger kids climb the ladders and ride the Genies. He'd gotten to ride the Genie, a workman's hand on his shoulder as they went up. He'd put his mother's big cat on a high branch sticking out at an odd angle, eye level with the brontosaurus. He'd rested it so that it looked like it was rearing up on its hind legs. His mother had stood below him, waving. They'd both been so happy, they'd walked the mile home in the rain.

Phil met them at the corner where Christine was getting a cab. He had Kitty in their Channel Thirteen tote bag. Steven couldn't believe he'd forgotten her.

"How're you doing?" Phil said. "Hanging in there?"

Steven didn't really feel like he needed to answer.

Phil held the bag.

"Oh," Christine said, looking worried. "I've got the dog," she said. "And I'm allergic." They all stood there for a minute, looking at Kitty in the bag. She looked back. Christine sneezed.

Phil looked surprised. "I didn't know you had a dog," he said. "Or that you were allergic."

Christine nodded. "Yeah. I am. I do. I am."

A cab slowed and then sped up again.

"Well, listen," Phil said. "He can come to my place. Sam's there." He smiled at Steven. "It'll be good for both of us."

Christine seemed willing to leave it up to Steven. His mom hadn't liked Christine all that much. He said Phil's was good. He took the tote bag from Phil and waited.

He didn't think Sam would be all that psyched about having him in her house. Sam was fifteen and a girl. She wasn't all that psyched about him period.

"I don't have any overnight stuff," he said.

Phil said, "You can borrow from Sam."

"Great," Steven said.

Christine put her arm around him. "Sorry," she said. She cried at everything. Once she cried at a commercial. "I'm so, so sorry," she said. She had her eye on a cab coming down Broadway.

Steven nodded.

"Okay then," she said, hailing the cab and wiping her eyes. "You call me if you need anything."

Phil took her place by Steven's side. Kitty squirmed around. The bag swayed and twisted. The cab pulled away.

Another one came. Phil held the door open.

"The address book," Steven said. "We gotta call people."

"I got it," Phil said.

"They let you take it?" Steven said.

"Get in," Phil said.

Steven took a step into the cab, then stepped back out. "I should get my toothbrush," he said.

Phil looked at him. "We've got to go," he said, not unkindly.

The driver peered at them over his shoulder.

"Sorry," Steven said.

"It's okay," Phil said, still holding the door open. Kitty meowed.

They got in. "A Hundred and eighth and Riverside," Phil told the driver. They were taking a cab six blocks. The driver pulled the meter on. Steven couldn't see his building anymore.

"We were supposed to watch nature shows," Steven said. "I should've been home earlier."

Phil was still looking at him.

"It's all my fault," Steven said.

"No," Phil said, so forcefully that he startled Steven. "No," he said again. "It's not."

Sam let him sleep in the top bunk. "It's just a bunk bed," she'd said. "I don't like them anymore. They're so elementary school."

Kitty sat on the pillow next to his head. She acted like she'd been sleeping there her whole life. There were little star- and moon-shaped pieces of paint missing from the ceiling. There was a small window next to him. Outside, he could hear the Riverside Drive traffic. He turned on his side and watched car lights. His first job had been walking the Rifkins' standard poodle. They'd given him a key; he'd gone over after school, letting himself into the empty house, waiting for the slow click of the old dog's nails on the hardwood floors. They'd walked to the park and back, only a block, but he'd felt important, a heavy leather leash in his hand, a real dog at the end of it.

Kitty stretched out and took over more of the pillow. The traffic light on 108th changed from red to green to yellow to red again. Phil's dad owned this building. Steven had never been able to understand why their apartment wasn't nicer or bigger.

Sam had *The Carpetbaggers* and a boxed set of Laura Ingalls Wilder books on the wide windowsill. The box looked like it hadn't been touched. There were posters and pictures of Baryshnikov and Mick Jagger on her walls. When she'd seen him noticing, she'd said, "I am so over the James Taylor thing." He hadn't known there was a James Taylor thing.

What would happen tomorrow? And the day after that? He wondered where the guy was right that second.

Sam turned over in the bunk below him. "Are you awake?" she asked.

"Yeah," he said.

"Can't sleep?" she said.

"Guess not," he said.

Phil had given him half a sleeping pill, but he wasn't feeling anything. He never had trouble sleeping. Maybe the pill had had some kind of reverse effect.

"What're you thinking about?" she asked. Then she said, "Sorry. Stupid question."

He squeezed his mother's keys hard enough to hurt. He wanted to answer. An image from last summer appeared: the tree swing his mother and he had come across in Riverside Park. The ropes looked too long to be swing ropes. His mother said she would push him. He sat, and she stood behind him and pulled him back as far as she could. He was worried he'd slip off. He was about to tell her he wanted to get off when she let go and he flew forward, his butt coming up off the seat a little. He made a small, surprised sound and she laughed.

Sam said, "Alcoholics say that it's a big deal when they've been sober longer than they were drunks," she said. "They, like, celebrate that day."

He tried to figure out what had made her say that.

"How do you know that?" he asked. The fan in the room was loudest when it rotated toward them. He had to time what he was saying.

"Phil's an alcoholic," she said. "I know a lot about them."

"I didn't know that," he said. "I mean about Phil," he said.

He could hear her moving around under her sheet. He was on top of his covers. Tweety and Sylvester. Kitty was lying across *I tawt I thaw a puddy tat. I did! I did!*

He was thinking about what Juan would say about him spending the night in Sam's room. Juan could go on about Sam. Steven told him he just liked her 'cause she was blond. "And," Juan had asked, "your point is?"

He had a hard-on. He got under the sheet. Kitty seemed annoyed.

"What're you doing?" Sam asked.

"Nothing," he said.

He was still hard. He put his mother's keys around himself.

"What are you doing?" Sam asked again.

"Nothing," he said.

"It better not be gross," she said.

"I took my mom's keys," he said.

She was quiet.

The door opened, and light from the hallway sliced into the room. Phil stood there, looking at them. Sam sighed loudly and made little sleepy noises. Steven kept his eyes open a crack. Against the light, Phil looked black. Steven wished he would quit looking at them. He felt like he might laugh. Sam murmured something. She was good, he thought. Maybe she was really asleep.

Phil came over to the bunks. He put his hand on Steven's belly. Steven tried to breathe evenly. Phil didn't seem upset. Steven's stomach rumbled.

"Phil?" Sam said.

"Hey, honey," he said. "Didn't mean to wake you." His voice didn't sound like his.

"What're you doing?" she asked.

"Nothing," he said, too loudly for the room. "Go to sleep." His fingers massaged Steven's belly lightly.

"You too," Sam said.

He took his hand away and pulled the sheet up over Steven a little more. "You're right," he said, leaning down to kiss her. "You're always right."

He left, closing the door behind him. The room went back to dark.

His hard-on had gone away and come back. "That was weird," he said.

"Sorry about him," Sam said. "Parents are mostly embarrassing, don't you think?"

Steven was quiet. He rubbed his flat hands up and down across the tops of his thighs. His skin was like he hadn't showered in weeks. His mother would've called him a Scoad Monster. He could hear her voice.

"God," Sam said. "I'm a major idiot."

What had the guy wanted? Why hadn't she given it to him?

"It wasn't her fault," Steven said. He hadn't meant to say it out loud.

Outside, a car alarm started and wouldn't stop. A dog barked. Someone told the dog to shut up.

"Of course it wasn't," Sam said. She sounded older than she was.

He imagined doing to the guy what he'd done to Steven's mother. Once, a friend of his mother's had been killed in a plane crash. "Imagine what those last few minutes were like?" his mother had said.

"What's your mom like?" he asked.

Sam started to talk and her words were like hands and he listened.

two

there are things to do when someone dies. He was surprised at breakfast when Phil had a list. He looked like he'd been up all night putting it together, but when Steven glanced at it, it was just a list of numbers, one through eight, with nothing next to them.

Getting woken up by Sam had been nice. He'd heard the sounds of her getting ready for her day. She hadn't been trying to wake him up. That had been the best part.

"You grind your teeth," she'd said.

He'd rolled his tongue around his gums, the insides of his cheeks. Sometimes he ground so hard his gums bled.

It was ten after nine. His mother would've said, sitting at the kitchen table, "What's the plan, little man?" She would've smiled at her own rhyme.

He couldn't stop thinking like this.

He threw up the Frosted Flakes and milk on the kitchen floor. He didn't know where their garbage can was. He kept his hand over his mouth even though he could feel nothing else was coming up. He couldn't look at them.

"Oh, man," Sam said.

She was being nice. But he hated her anyway.

Phil said her name like a warning. He told Steven it didn't matter, and led him to the bathroom off the kitchen. The bathroom was about four steps from where he'd puked.

In the small space, Phil's smell got to him. He told him he could handle it from there. He tried to sound normal while holding his breath. He tried not to swallow. Phil left. Steven ran both taps full blast and flushed the toilet and rinsed his mouth with the cold water and closed his eyes so he wouldn't see bits of anything making their way down the drain.

His mother would've held his bangs away from his head. He threw up a lot. *Sensitive* was the word people who liked him used.

He could hear Phil moving around in the kitchen. Sam said something. Phil didn't answer.

Steven sat under the tiny sink, his shoulder wedged under one of the pipes. From now on, when he thought of his mother, he would think of the hallway rug bunched up under her hip. Somewhere, the guy was eating breakfast. Or maybe not even up yet.

He stood up and looked at himself in the mirror. "Pussy," he said.

Steam from the hot water was filling the little room. The mirror got cloudy. He made a fist and put it under the hot water. It got red. He counted fifty and turned the water off, putting his hand in his pocket before going back out.

The autopsy was going to take a little time. Phil was talking to Detective McGuire. Steven was listening on the extension in Sam's room. She was digging around in her closet, pretending not to notice. She had a dark red phone. She had to pay her own phone bill out of her allowance. She'd had a checking account since she was twelve. She cooked dinner one night a week. Phil said he wanted her to be able to take care of herself.

He'd argued about it with Steven's mother. He said she coddled Steven. "You're not helping him in the long run," Steven had heard him say to her more than once. "What's he gonna do when you're not around?"

Phil hadn't meant anything by it. Still, it was freaky.

Detective McGuire told Phil that they should just make their arrangements, do what needed to be done. The cops would need to keep the apartment stationary for another forty-eight hours, but after that, it was all theirs.

Sam backed out of the closet on all fours, dragging a cardboard box. She looked pleased with herself until she saw him. Then she looked something else.

Phil was asking about the guy. Were there leads? Theories? Anything?

Detective McGuire said the case was a priority. They were on it. They'd know more after the autopsy. They were working on phone records. It looked like she might have made a phone call.

"A phone call?" Phil repeated. "While the guy was in the apartment? Isn't that a little weird?"

"Yes," Detective McGuire said. "A little."

"Who did she call?" Phil asked.

"We're working on it," McGuire said. "On all of this. Listen," he said, "in New York these things take longer than they should. I'll let you know when the body becomes available."

Phil asked if any determination had been made about—he interrupted himself to clear his throat, and then finished his sentence—sexual assault. He wanted to know about sexual assault.

It was like last spring when Juan had found a note about Steven that a girl he liked had written to a friend, and had offered it to him to read.

The detective said they wouldn't know about that until after the autopsy. It was a good bet, though, he said.

Steven wondered how cops knew what they knew.

"How's the kid?" Detective McGuire asked, like it had taken him this long to get the courage up.

Sam looked at him and then left the room. Phil took a breath like he'd hoped he'd get through this conversation without that. Steven pressed the disconnect button. That was the way you did it if you didn't want to get caught. The fan turned back and forth, back and forth. Hot air moved around him. Kitty wove around his ankles, meowing. He held the receiver down to her and she rubbed her cheek against it like it was what she'd been looking for.

When Phil came to the doorway, Steven still had the receiver in his hand. Phil took in the scene.

"You heard?" he asked.

Steven nodded.

Phil gestured at the cardboard box. "Sam says those will fit you," he said.

"Where is she?" Steven asked.

"Music," he said.

She played piano. One time when they'd all been over here, his mother had played her guitar, Sam played the piano, and he'd played drums with chopsticks on an overturned box. Beatles songs.

He dragged the box over. In Sam's handwriting on the top flap it said 12–13 YEARS in black marker. He opened the box and peered inside. "There's a lot of purple," he said.

Phil smiled. "Boys wear purple," he said.

Steven didn't say anything.

Phil considered him. "Well, see what else you can find. We can always go over to Morris Brothers."

"That's okay," Steven said. "This is good."

He chose a pair of navy blue gym shorts and a homemade T-shirt that said DERVISH POWER. They seemed like the least girlie things in the box.

"I borrowed some of your socks," he said. He'd pulled them up to his knees. The heel came to the middle of his calf.

"No problem," Phil said. "Did you get them from the basket in the closet? Those are the clean ones."

"You have the same sneakers as the guy," Steven said.

Phil stared. "I'm sorry," he said.

Steven shrugged. "Everyone does," he said.

They didn't seem to have anything more to say to one another.

"Ready to make some calls?" Phil asked after a while.

They sat at the kitchen counter and glanced at the open address book. There were cross-outs and eraser marks. Things were written in pen and pencil. All in her handwriting. It was tiny and looked like it should only appear on small pieces of very thin paper.

He studied the page hard to keep from crying. Lisa Altiere. Becky Amidon. Josh Armstrong. Who were these people? He felt like he'd felt that time a few years ago when he'd come out of his bedroom to get something to eat, and his mother was in the living room on the couch with her feet in a guy's lap. He'd never seen the guy before. Kurt. His name was Kurt.

He looked at Phil. Phil was crying.

"We probably shouldn't go in alphabetical order," Steven said.

Phil looked at him like he had no idea what he was talking about but was willing to hear him out.

"There are probably people we should start with," Steven said. Phil nodded.

"Probably my dad," Steven said after a minute.

Phil nodded again. He flipped to the *E*s. There was the number. They stared at it.

"He may not be there," Steven said. "Those guys called him last night. He said he was coming here today."

If they didn't call, he wondered how long it would take for his father to call him.

"I guess we should call anyway," Steven said.

It was like talking to himself. Like the part of Phil that was a grown-up had decided to leave. He nodded again, got up, took his coffee, and left the room. He was crying the whole time.

Steven checked the clock. It had twelve different versions of yellow smiley faces instead of numbers. It was noon. In San Diego that was nine. He knew that much. If his father was still there, he would be at work. His father was a plastic surgeon. His mother said that was the main reason she'd left him. She'd put him through medical school. He was supposed to be some other kind of doctor, something better than a plastic surgeon. But somewhere along the way he'd changed his mind and become someone his mother barely recognized. He had a wife in San Diego. Kids. A boy and a girl. Steven didn't know their names. They were little. He guessed the whole plastic surgeon thing didn't bother the other wife. He didn't see what was wrong with plastic surgery. His father probably gave people who never looked in mirrors a chance. Once, he'd heard Mrs. Carpanetti tell his mom that not all doctors had to run free clinics in Harlem.

The new wife had made it part of their marriage agreement that she'd never have to take care of Steven. He wasn't supposed to know that, but he overheard his mother talking about it with a guy one night.

He thought of her feet in Kurt's lap. He wondered if she ever thought she and his father had done the wrong thing. He wondered if she'd been happy.

He dialed. Then he had to go to the bathroom. He had diarrhea. He stayed in there a long time. Blood rushed to his head and stayed there.

Back at the counter, he opened a can of ginger ale and dialed again. The woman who answered sounded like there wasn't a problem she couldn't fix.

He asked to speak to Dr. Engel.

She said he was with a patient; if there was a message, she'd be happy to pass it on. Who should she say was calling? She was merry.

"His son," Steven said.

She was quiet. His son, she was probably thinking, was way too little to be making phone calls, to be sounding like this boy.

"His other son," he said, helping out.

She was still quiet. He couldn't tell if she knew about him or not.

She told him to hang on.

The phone played jazz. His mother had said his father used to take her to listen to music in the Village. They'd heard Tiny Tim sing "Tiptoe Through the Tulips." Steven hadn't been impressed, and his mother had scrunched her face at him. "Whadda *you* know?" she'd said, smiling.

There he was. Right on the other end of the phone, saying, "Hello?" just like he was supposed to.

"Hi," he said. He didn't know what to call him. "It's me."

His father didn't say anything.

"Steven," he added.

"I know," he said.

Steven wasn't good at talking with grown-ups.

"She's dead," he said for the first time ever. "Last night." He said these things though he knew his father already knew.

"I know," he said quietly. "The police called."

"I found her," Steven said. He saw her again, lying there. He saw her face again. He felt as if he were standing at the edge of something high. Would thinking of her be like this from now on?

His father was quiet for a long time. Steven didn't know what else to say.

"I'll be there tonight," he said, and Steven thought he might cry. He wanted so much for his father to be someone he'd like. He wanted even more for his father to be someone who liked him.

Steven gave him Phil's number, and his father said he'd see him tomorrow, and they hung up. He sat there at the kitchen counter, his hand on the phone, not feeling like throwing up at all.

Phil called everyone else.

three

detective McGuire called and wanted to talk to him. Phil handed the phone over and stood there next to him.

"So," McGuire said. "How're you doing? Get any sleep?"

"Some," Steven said.

"I need you to come down to the precinct," he said. "I need your help on something."

"What is it?" Steven asked.

"I'll explain when you get here," he said. "Don't worry," he added.

"What?" Phil mouthed.

Steven shrugged.

"Sorry," McGuire said. "You're our go-to guy," he said.

"Okay," Steven said. "Now?" he asked.

"Whenever," McGuire said. "Today. Soon. Now is good," he said.

"Okay," Steven said again. He waited.

Then McGuire said, "I guess Miss Mahoney didn't work out."

Phil was standing in front of him. He held his hand out for the phone.

"It might be better," McGuire said, "if you could come down by yourself."

Steven looked at Phil. He still had his hand out. Phil had lied about knowing about Christine's allergies. Steven remembered him suggesting a hypnotist; the guy had cured him of his fear of flying and his three-pack-a-day smoking habit. Christine should try him for her allergies.

Steven handed him the phone.

He'd been to the 24th Precinct twice before. Once to register his bike and once to report it stolen. It was a gold Raleigh ten-speed. His mother had made him a deal. She'd buy it for him, but he had to work off half of it. Mom's Layaway, she called it. He'd thought the whole plan was unfair. She hadn't even taught him how to ride a bike. She'd tried, on the sidewalk in front of their building, but he'd kept falling off, scraping up his legs and arms, yelling at her, so she'd told him to forget it, she wasn't going through *that* again. One of her guy friends had taught him. The one Steven had introduced her to; the guy who'd helped him out that day he'd been lost. He'd been around off and on for a few months. One of the college kids. He had an old sports car and looked like he was trying to stare into the sun. He had an accent. In stores, he always joked about what Steven was going to buy him. It bothered Steven that he couldn't remember the guy's name. Steven had had some hopes for him.

The three of them went to the field in the park that had a slope at one end. The guy told him to keep his feet off the pedals. The bike they used was purple, with a banana seat. It was too small, but the guy said that would make things easier. He set Steven up at the top of the slope and then let him go. It was hard to keep his feet away from the pedals, and he fell a lot. It felt like those dreams he sometimes had of trying to run down a flight of stairs too quickly. His mom watched from the bottom of the hill. The guy told him to aim for her. Steven was embarrassed when people noticed them. When Steven made it all the way down without falling, the guy clapped loudly twice. On his last ride, Steven kept pedaling, past his mother, off the grass onto the asphalt basketball court. He circled, his hands tingling from gripping the handlebars. He stopped across the court and watched her. The guy was walking over. In a minute, he'd hug her from behind and she'd turn to smile and thank him. She was laughing her real laugh. He started pedaling again. He circled in front of her. "It's as good as I thought it would be," he told her. "I'm glad," she said.

Manuel kept the Raleigh in the building's laundry room until Steven had done enough dishes, set enough tables, folded enough laundry. When Manuel brought it up Steven and his mom were waiting in the hallway, and when the elevator doors opened it was like they'd both won a prize.

It got stolen a few months after that from outside the Burger King on Broadway. Juan had ridden Steven home on his handlebars. Steven hadn't used his lock, but when his mother asked, Juan lied for him.

The station was as ratty as he remembered it. Fluorescent lights and paper cups, water coolers making their sounds. Out-of-date flyers on bulletin boards. Wanted people. Missing cats. Stolen bikes. An old man cop behind Plexiglas with a little hole in it. He didn't want to think about what they'd found. Sometimes he felt like his whole life was a pile of things he didn't want to think about.

Detective McGuire came down the stairs. It looked like he hadn't changed his clothes. He had his eye on Phil the whole way over. He came right up to him, hand outstretched, like Phil was the guy he'd asked to see. When he finally looked at Steven, Steven felt himself get hot, but all McGuire said was, "Hey, bud. Good to see you again."

"I told him I was supposed to come alone," Steven said.

"I didn't think that was a good idea," Phil said.

McGuire shrugged. "Not a problem," he said, but he hadn't stopped watching Phil.

He took them into a small room with a table and four chairs. There was a shoebox-looking thing on the table. Out the window Steven could see the tops of the trees on 100th Street. The windows had built-in wire.

Panty hose had been inside her pants. They needed to know if either of them knew if they were hers.

"Inside her pants," Phil repeated.

"What does that mean?" Steven asked.

Phil couldn't look at him. McGuire was sweeping him with his eyes in a slow, regular way, like he was following a hypnotist's watch, like it was a system he had worked out. Once, Steven and his mother had borrowed Manuel's metal detector and gone to Coney Island. It was like that.

McGuire cleared his throat. "Rolled up," he said. His hands

moved unhelpfully in the air. "Placed," he said, "within her under-garments."

They were all staring at the box.

"Okay?" McGuire said, putting his hand on the box and looking at Steven.

Steven nodded.

McGuire opened the box and took out a plastic bag with the panty hose inside. His mother hated panty hose, especially in the summer. She was supposed to wear them to work, but sometimes she just shaved really well and oiled her legs with lotion and kept them a little tan. She used to sit in her window with her legs dangling over the edge to keep her tan up.

When she did have to wear them, she started taking them off even before she walked in the door. Sometimes she hopped the last few steps into the apartment, pulling them off one foot and then the other.

McGuire laid the bag out on the table like he was a salesman.

"They're hers," Steven said.

Phil was surprised. "How do you know?" he said.

Steven pointed at the wide lace waistband that dipped in front. "She said she liked how this kind didn't dig into her tummy."

Someone opened the door, looked in, and closed it again.

Steven looked at the panty hose, trying to smell them from where he was sitting. Her work clothes always smelled a little sweaty. It was hard work, she said, taking care of everyone.

McGuire asked if he remembered if she'd been wearing them the day before.

He tried to think. She'd been drinking coffee at the kitchen table when he'd left for Juan's. When he tried to imagine what she'd been wearing at the beginning of the day, all he could see was that bunched-up dress. Something bitter worked its way into his throat.

"If she was going to work, maybe," he said. "If she wasn't, then no."

They kept looking at him.

"I can't remember if she was supposed to go to work," he said. "Her shifts were always changing."

He looked at them. He shrugged. A scuffle seemed to be going on in the hallway.

McGuire glanced at the door. "I better go see what's up," he said, standing.

Phil said, "She was supposed to go to work. She was supposed to work eleven to seven. Come home. Have dinner with her son. Get ready to go out for ice cream. She was supposed to go out for ice cream." He looked up at the detective. "You don't even know whether she got to work or not?" He stood up a little, but kept his knees bent, like he might sit down again at any minute. "What *have* you been doing? What *do* you know?"

Steven didn't like it when grown-ups argued. He didn't know he was supposed to have been home for dinner. He didn't know about the ice cream. If he'd come home for dinner, maybe none of this would've happened.

McGuire looked genuinely sad. Something hard hit the other side of the door. Someone told someone else to take it easy.

"I'm on your side," he said. "I really am."

Steven believed him.

"She went to work. She came home," McGuire said. "She got the mail. She didn't make dinner."

Steven interrupted him. "If I wasn't around, she usually didn't eat," he said.

"We know what we know," McGuire said. "We're just trying to know more."

He told them to sit tight. When he opened the door, whatever had been going on out there seemed to have disappeared. A woman officer walked by with a big stack of folders. McGuire gave them the "one minute" sign with his finger and closed the door behind him.

They sat there, the panty hose in their little bag between them.

McGuire came back in. He wanted to know about Mrs. Carpanetti and her son, from upstairs.

"What about them?" Steven asked.

McGuire shrugged. "You know, whatever. Are you friends? What're they like?"

They'd been around forever. They lived upstairs. For a couple of years, Michael and Steven had done stuff together, stuff that made Steven embarrassed to think about. And then, when Steven was ten, it had stopped. "They're good," he said.

"Was your mother friends with them?" McGuire asked.

She didn't like how much time he spent with Michael, but she didn't have anything better for him to do, so mostly she'd left them alone, warning him sometimes not to be stupid. "She liked them okay," he said. "They weren't really *friends*. Sometimes they watered our plants and stuff."

McGuire wrote something down.

"Did you and them have a regular Tuesday thing?" he asked.

Steven didn't know what he meant, and then remembered the nature shows. His mother couldn't believe the things he forgot.

"Yeah," he said. "Nature shows. But I stayed out late with Juan."

McGuire nodded. "All righty," he said.

He had one more question. Had either of them seen her address book?

Phil frowned a little, like he was working hard on the problem.

McGuire was watching them.

"Phil has it," Steven said.

No one said anything for a minute. Phil was still frowning.

"We took it to make some phone calls," Phil said.

"I didn't take it," Steven said.

They both looked at him. It was the kind of quiet that was really loud.

McGuire nodded. "I figured there was an easy explanation," he said. "There usually is."

He put his hand on Steven's shoulder. "Let me have a minute," he said. To Phil, he said, "Why don't you have a seat by my desk. I'll be with you shortly."

He got up and held the door open for Phil. There was a uniform guy waiting there. Steven looked out the window. Phil told the detective sure, no problem, and only glanced at Steven before leaving the room.

He had the afternoon to himself. He spent it poking around Sam's room, trying to come up with details that Juan would like. She hid her diary in her underwear drawer. It seemed kind of unimaginative. Her closet was filled with labeled boxes and file folders. She had a shoe rack and a special hanger for belts.

He found an old pack of red modeling clay and warmed it and worked it as he slid open drawers and checked under the bed. The dye of the clay came off on his hands. He made a series of little monsters. One with an open mouth and bug eyes. One with a hat. Years ago, he'd made, and tried to sell around the neighborhood, his Tiny Terrors Series. Tiny versions of famous villains. His mother still had his Phantom of the Opera and his Creature from the Black Lagoon on the kitchen windowsill.

He made a final curled, sleeping monster, and lined them all up on Sam's desk. Maybe she would like them. He washed his hands, found a pair of drumsticks in a box marked INSTRUMENTS, and for the rest of the afternoon, drummed along to her record collection.

His father didn't take him to a restaurant. They took a taxi all the way to Forty-ninth and First. There was a tiny store on a part of First Avenue that slanted downhill. Harry's Chicken. The left side of the sign was about two feet lower than the right. In the tiny window, you could see Harry cooking chickens on a grill that took up half the store.

His father was excited. He hadn't been here for three or four years. He wondered if Harry would remember him. It was the best chicken in the city. You couldn't get stuff like this in San Diego.

Like chicken? Steven thought. Then he thought, four years. He'd been eight. He tried to decide how weird he thought it was that his father was thinking about chicken. He remembered his mother saying something about his father being at his best when he was eating or talking about eating. She said it was a thing Jews and Italians had in common. That and fights. And the belief that actions had consequences. And guilt. Those last two, she said, were connected.

Harry remembered him. Harry wore thick black glasses and white butcher clothes and one of those white paper soda jerk hats. He had grease stains all over his apron. He was missing a lot of teeth. The few he had were crooked. Steven liked him.

They took the chicken and the sides of cole slaw and potato salad to a park his father knew on the East River. There were trees, but it was mostly concrete, shaped to fit between the buildings and the FDR Drive. It was all fenced in, down at the bottom of a long set of black stone stairs. People were letting their dogs run around without leashes.

His father picked a bench. Rush hour traffic crawled behind them. There was a thick, hot breeze off the river.

"God, that feels good," his father said.

The dogs were interested in the chicken. Every now and then, his father threw a piece to one of them. It didn't seem like a smart thing to do.

His father looked like him. He hadn't expected that. Their hair was the same straight brown kind. Ringo hair, his mother called it. His father was wearing jeans and a Dodgers T-shirt. He didn't seem like the guy Steven's mother had sometimes described.

"Do you have a dog?" Steven asked.

His father nodded. "Two." He wiped his hands on a napkin and passed Steven a few. "Brother and sister. We got them when the twins were born."

Steven figured that for a while everything he said was going to hurt.

There was a doorman standing at the wall at the top of the stairs. His uniform was nicer than Manuel's. Manuel didn't really have one. Sometimes he wore a shirt with his name on it.

Manuel liked Steven and his mother. He did stuff for them without their asking. Once he'd helped make Steven's Halloween costume.

He rolled his father's name over in his mind. Benjamin Engel. Benjamin. Ben.

"What happens now?" he asked.

His father sighed and rubbed his thighs like he was rolling out clay. It was something Steven did too.

"Well, I talked with the detectives today, and I'll talk to them again tomorrow. I got to tell you, though, it doesn't seem like they've got much to go on." He smiled. His front tooth was chipped. "We're all doing what we can," he said.

Steven flashed on the guy running down the street. White T-shirt. Jeans. White socks. Green and white Adidas.

Most of the dogs were leaving. They climbed the stairs like a parade. The doorman opened the gate at the top with a flourish and a bow. One by one the dogs licked his face.

"I meant about me," Steven said. He hated his father for misunderstanding. He hated himself for not being able to just keep quiet.

His father twisted his wedding ring around his finger. "Of course you did," he said. "Sorry."

"It's okay," Steven said.

The park smelled of dog poop and car fumes. He couldn't smell the water. He held his greasy fingers up to his nose.

"You'll come live with me and Trish and the twins," his father said.

He said the twins would love having an older brother, but he'd taken too long to answer, and he wouldn't look Steven in the eye, and Steven knew that whatever it was he'd been waiting to hear his father say, this wasn't it.

His father reached into his back pocket and pulled out his wallet. "Do you want to see some pictures?" he asked.

"Not really," Steven said.

His father seemed hurt. "Okay," he said. He held the wallet in both hands like an egg.

When Steven got back, Sam was hanging out the doorway of her room, listening to Phil in his bedroom. She saw Steven at the end of the hall and gestured him down, holding a finger to her lips like a kindergarten teacher.

He stood next to her. Her hair touched his bare arm. She pointed at her father's partially open door and mimed a phone to her ear. He nodded. She looked at him. "Nice shirt," she mouthed.

"I don't know his name," Phil was saying.

"Yes," he said.

"She told me about him," he said.

"She wasn't seeing him anymore," he said. He sounded annoyed.

Sam was chewing on a strand of her hair. The blond got darker when it got wet. He tried to figure out which boyfriend Phil could be talking about. Kitty appeared, making figure eights around their legs. "Meow," Sam said to her quietly. "Me. Ow."

"Yes, I'm certain," Phil said. He sounded more annoyed.

Steven's head was hot. He leaned it against the door frame. He'd read a murder mystery about a woman who'd been stabbed. At the crime scene, to find out the time of death, they'd stuck a meat thermometer into her liver.

Sam took him by the shoulders and steered him into her room and onto her beanbag. She closed the door and came back over. She sat on her heels, staring at him.

He felt folded over. Sometimes his mother used to carry him with his back to her front, holding him under his knees. His knees would be up by his nose. She'd carry him like that until he started to slip. It always felt good and bad to be let go. He closed his eyes and pushed his eyelids around over them.

"Do you need something?" Sam whispered.

He nodded.

She waited.

He didn't know what to ask for.

She put a hand on his knee. He kept his eyes closed and asked her to leave. She only hesitated a minute before she did, closing the door behind her.

Later, when he asked her what she thought her father had been talking about, she didn't try to avoid the question, and he was glad for that. She figured they were talking about the guy his mother had been seeing a few months back. She didn't know anything about him, just that her dad had been upset, and then he hadn't been anymore, and she'd figured they'd worked it out.

The thing Steven was most glad about was that she didn't say a thing about his not knowing. She didn't say he should've known; she didn't say there was no way he could've known.

"I don't know anything about anything," he said.

She was quiet for a minute and then she snorted. "Grown-ups," she said. "Who wants to know anything about them?"

four

Juan came with him. They used the fire escape and waited until they knew Manuel would be in his apartment at the back of the building eating his lunch and watching his soap operas.

The metal of the fire escape was so hot he wished he'd brought gloves. He wrapped each ladder rung in the bottom of his T-shirt until Juan looked up from behind him and said, "Dude. What're you doing?"

Steven opened the window that had the lock that never worked, and they crawled on their bellies over the flaking paint of the sill, through the orange curtains, into his mother's bedroom. He couldn't believe it had taken him this long to remember her diaries.

They stood up, brushing paint flakes off themselves. Juan asked if this was the window the guy had used.

"How'd you know about that?" Steven asked.

He shrugged. "Everyone's talking," he said.

Steven's surprise was stupid. "What're they saying?" he asked. He wasn't even sure who "they" were.

Juan ran his hand over his short tight hair a few times. "Every-thing," he said.

Steven pictured all their friends at the side entrance of the mu-seum. There were big double-sided stairs going up to a landing where there was supposed to have been a café, but then something had happened. So there was nothing but a wall that was good for leaning against that hid you from the people down below.

Summers, they went there almost every night. Steven didn't hang out with the group as much as Juan did. He wasn't so good at groups. Juan was the only reason Steven knew the other kids. And Juan was the only reason the other kids paid any attention to Steven.

Juan surveyed the bedroom. "Where are they?" he asked.

"I don't know," Steven said. "I could never find them."

"You know we can't, like, *hang out* here," Juan said. "I thought this was a more in-and-out kinda thing."

Everything was the same. Another forty-eight hours, McGuire had said. It was still a crime scene. Someone had pulled all the cur-tains. The windows were shut. Outside it was midday; hazy light too bright to look at straight. Inside it was dim and stale.

"I think in here," Steven said, looking around vaguely. He didn't really want to go back out to the hall.

"You think?" Juan said, but he got on his hands and knees and looked under the bed. "Oh, man," he said. "Bring on the Elec-trolux."

Mrs. Carpanetti was thumping around upstairs.

The elevator gears ground to a halt. Each sound made him jump, not out of fear but out of anticipation. Here she comes, he found himself thinking.

What would he say to her? Hi. I missed you. What happened? What happened?

He spread out on his belly next to Juan on the floor and looked under the bed. There were her good work shoes, the ones that were still white. Some Legos. Some cigarette butts. She pretended she didn't smoke. When she didn't have time to throw them out the window or flush them down the toilet, she crushed them out and threw them under the bed. There were always sticks of incense stuck in their plants. She was always lighting scented candles. He could tell how much she'd been drinking by how many cigarette butts he found the next day.

"She was good at cleaning the stuff you could see," he said. She was a single mom, she said. People expected her to let things slide.

The top of her dresser was always out of a magazine. The bathroom sink was always wiped. She cleaned the kitty litter twice a day. Inside, her drawers were like small explosions. There was a utility drawer in the kitchen that they could open only three inches. Enough to see the jumble of tools and twine and take-out menus. Enough to see the piece of the garlic press that was keeping the thing jammed.

He'd told Juan they were looking for anything about this other guy Phil had been talking about. Letters maybe, or a photo even. But what he'd really come back for were her journals. She'd kept them for years. She'd tried to get him to keep his own. When he was too young to write, she'd take dictation. "What did you do today?" she'd ask, and she'd write his answers in her tiny, clear handwriting.

Every year she bought him a new journal, but he'd never been good at it, and he'd quit before filling up one book.

She talked about hers, and made clear how important they were by never letting him find out where she kept them.

Even if what was in them didn't help the detectives at all, he wanted them. He wanted to know what else he'd missed.

In one of the photos on her dresser he was eating cake on his first birthday. In one she was wearing that silly hat, swinging from a NO PARKING sign like Gene Kelly. They didn't have many of the two of them together. He was already having trouble remembering her voice. He thought the journals might help.

the blood in the hallway and the front hall had dried. They stood over the spot. The heat in the living room was like the air under a blanket.

"Man," Juan said.

He looked over. "What's it like?" he said. "What's it feel like?"

Steven was glad he'd asked. "I don't know," Steven said. "I really don't know."

But after Juan went in the kitchen, Steven stood there thinking that in a couple of years, maybe even less, people who lived here wouldn't even know what had happened.

they found a small stack of letters rubber-banded together in a duffel bag in the hall closet, but no journals. They were checking the bedroom one last time when they heard the front door open. He recognized the jangle of Manuel's keys. They heard him say, "I shouldn't be doing this," and they heard another guy say something like, "I owe you."

They slid out the window as quietly as they could, leaving it open. They took the fire escape stairs two at a time, slid down the ladder like firemen, and were running before they hit the ground.

Even when it was clear no one was following, even when they'd been walking, not running, for blocks, Juan was practically bouncing off the ground. He was walking on his toes. "*That was the guy,*" he said again. He'd been saying that or something like it since they'd slowed down.

"We don't know that," Steven said.

He was trying to hear the guy's voice again. Had he recognized it? He couldn't tell.

Juan looked at him. "You *know* it was him. Did you recognize the voice?"

"No," Steven said.

"Think," Juan said.

"I *am,*" Steven said.

"Why you think he's coming back?" he asked. He was more talking to himself.

Steven had asked himself the same question. Was there something in the apartment he wanted? Needed? Evidence he needed to get rid of? He could just be sick. Steven thought about the panty hose.

"We should call the police," Juan said.

"I *know,*" Steven said.

"He could still be there," Juan said.

"I know," Steven said. "He's probably not there anymore," he said.

Juan said, "This is getting major."

It was already major, Steven thought. The first thing was the big rock into the pond; everything else was ripples.

When they got back to Juan's, his mom looked at them and said, "What's the matter with you two?"

"Nothing," Juan said. "It's hot," he said.

You could see her deciding to let it go.

Steven caught Juan's eye. Juan looked down. The guy could still be in the apartment, and they weren't going to call anyone. Juan wanted to. If it were up to him, they would. Steven understood he was the kind of person who made best friends do the wrong thing.

Juan's mother handed Steven an envelope. It was small, like an invitation, and there was no stamp or address, just his name in small block letters.

"It was in the mailbox," she said, and then she waited.

Inside was the picture half of a notecard. The edge had that fuzzy, torn by hand look. The picture was an overhead view of a bamboo steamer bowl of dumplings with a pair of chopsticks next to it. On the back, in the same block letters, it said, "Hope you're doing okay."

Juan and his mom peered over Steven's shoulder. "No signature?" she said. She was trying to make her voice sound normal. It didn't.

Steven shook his head. Even that felt like he was doing it wrong.

Juan was up on his toes again. "It's him," he said, glancing at Steven. "Who knows you're here?"

Steven put the card back in the envelope. "Uh, everyone," he said. Since McGuire had suggested Steven stay here instead of at either Phil *or* Christine's, he'd called twice; Steven's father had called once, and Phil had called four or five times, each time more worked up about McGuire's decision to make other living arrangements for Steven.

"It's from Detective McGuire," Steven said.

They both looked at him.

"We were talking about Chinese food," Steven said. His mother called him Glass Head because of what a bad liar he was.

Juan's mom smiled like she was willing to believe whatever he wanted her to believe, but when she took his head in her hands and kissed him on the forehead, she said into his hair, "I don't think so, little man. Let's call the detectives."

In Juan's house, animals ran free. There were a lot of them. You watched the floor, checked chairs and sofas, shook out shoes.

When McGuire rang the doorbell, Juan shooed the guinea pig away from the front door with his foot. Steven put the iguana in the large palm, and Juan's mom held her arms up for the parakeets. She looked like someone doing a victory lap.

Steven figured McGuire had seen stranger things.

He looked pleased to see Steven. He was sweaty. Steven was glad he was there. All Steven had to do was tell him everything he knew and watch him go to work.

They sat in the living room. Juan's mom liked plants, and Steven figured she wanted the living room to look like one of her paintings. She'd moved all the furniture away from the walls a couple of feet and surrounded them with plants.

McGuire sat on the couch, studying the notecard and the envelope. Every now and then the ficas tree dropped a leaf on him. He sighed and fit the card back in the envelope, put all of it into a plastic bag, and slid it into his jacket pocket.

"We gotta talk," he said.

Where should he start? Steven thought. Breaking into a crime scene? Hearing voices? Getting this note?

When had all this become his responsibility? He remembered his mother standing in his room asking if he wanted to watch TV with her. "No," he'd said, not looking up.

Two of the gerbils chased each other around McGuire's feet and then disappeared under the couch.

"The results of the autopsy are in," McGuire said.

But when McGuire said what he had to say, it was like Steven had known all along, and hearing the words out loud in someone else's voice made him feel better, not worse, and he could sit up again.

"There were what we call hilt marks around the wounds," McGuire said. "Did you and your mom have any kind of thin serrated knife with a kind of hilt on it? Maybe a steak knife?"

It helped to be concentrating on something specific. "In the basket on the table in the front hall," Steven said. "She used it to open packages."

"Anywhere else she might've kept it?" McGuire asked.

Steven didn't know.

McGuire was going to put a uniform guy on him. The card was probably nothing, but they wanted to make clear to this guy that having anything at all to do with Steven wasn't a good idea.

"Help me out here," he said. "Who's got an interest in you and your mom?"

Steven could hear Juan and his mom trying to be quiet in the bedroom. Last spring, Steven had locked himself out of the apartment, and he'd had to go to the bathroom, and he'd gone one flight down on the service stairs and taken a dump on the landing. He didn't know why he was thinking about that now.

"I told you which bar she liked," he said. "I told you who had the address book."

McGuire nodded, like he'd already written those down. "You did," he said. "You did. But here's what I'm thinking. If you tell me about that bar, it might be because you have a reason to tell me about that bar. The address book—same thing." He watched Steven. "See what I'm saying?"

The air conditioner kicked on. "I don't know why I told you those things," he said.

McGuire nodded. "Think," he said.

Why had he told him about Phil taking the address book? Did he really think Phil could've done those things to his mother? He tried to remember the voice in the apartment. Three words that he wasn't even sure he'd heard right. Had it been Phil?

"Somebody raped and stabbed your mother," McGuire said. "Now is not the time for bits and pieces. Everything you know, guy. No more, no less."

Steven went to Juan's room and got the letters out of his sleeping bag. He hadn't even looked at them yet. He handed them over.

"Where'd you get these?" McGuire asked.

"I went to the apartment," Steven said.

"You went to the apartment," McGuire said. "D'you go with Tonto?" he asked, tilting his head toward the bedroom.

"No," Steven said. He didn't want to get Juan in trouble.

McGuire raised his eyebrows.

"Yes," Steven said. "But it was my idea."

"Congratulations," McGuire said. "How'd you get in?"

If he could answer one question at a time, he thought he might be able to tell him everything. "Through the bedroom window. The lock doesn't work. It never has," he said.

McGuire pinched the end of his nose a few times, like it was running. "Through the window," he said. "Breaking into a crime scene," he said. "Are you listening to this?" he said.

Steven couldn't tell if he was talking to him. It didn't feel like he had relieved himself of anything. The more he told him, the bigger the whole problem seemed to get.

"Listen," McGuire said. "I'm not gonna tell you what I think about your own little detective agency. You know what there is to think about that. You wanna do something? You wanna be involved? Start doing something that's gonna help."

Now Steven was crying. "I don't want to do anything," he said.

McGuire seemed not to notice. "She was your mother," he said. "You're involved. And you've been making choices all over the place. Doing; not doing. They've all got consequences," he said.

Steven sat there while McGuire read through the letters. At first he concentrated on crying. Then he concentrated on not crying.

"I was looking for her journals," he said. "She kept journals."

McGuire stopped reading. "D'you find them?" he asked.

Steven shook his head. Tell him about the voices, he thought. I heard a guy, he imagined saying. He went over what he knew. There was a guy in the apartment. Manuel let him in. It had to be someone Manuel knew. It had to be someone Manuel trusted. Phil, he thought. Anyone.

Tell him what you know, he thought. *Tell him what you know and let him answer the questions. It's his job. He's trained for it.*

"Why would anyone care about me?" Steven asked.

McGuire kept his place on the letter with a finger. "I don't know. You tell me."

Why wasn't he telling McGuire about Manuel and the guy? In school last year, five of the girls had gotten an unsigned letter. The person who'd written it made fun of them, listed their flaws. The person imagined lining them up and shooting them. Steven had had an idea of who the person was, but when the teacher had talked to each of them privately, Steven had said he didn't know anything. Two of the girls, he really liked. They were friends.

McGuire finished the letters and restacked them. "Not much here," he said.

He stuck out his lower lip like he was thinking. "Listen," he said. "Why doncha keep the people you're hanging out with to a minimum." He tapped the letters against his thigh. "I wouldn't spend any time with Phil if I were you," he said.

"Why?" Steven said. "Is there something you want to tell me about Phil?" It sounded like the kind of question McGuire would ask.

"No," he said. "Not really. But he's the boyfriend. He's interested in you. You do the math, Sherlock."

He stood. "Is there something *you* want to tell *me* about Phil?"

Steven didn't know what he thought about Phil anymore. He shook his head.

"Okay then," McGuire said.

He handed the letters back. "You might be interested in the one on top," he said. "Where's the john?" he asked.

Steven pointed, and McGuire palmed his head on his way by.

The letter was from Steven's father. It said she shouldn't worry, all boys, especially ones without fathers in the home, looked for male role models, and as far as he could tell from everything she'd told him, their boy was doing better than most.

The thought of them talking about him made him feel like laughing.

"Thanks," he said when McGuire came back.

"Don't thank me," he said. "He's your dad."

His father came to Juan's for dinner. Juan's mom made Greek stuff, like he was someone special. Juan's dad got out the good glasses and offered his father the whiskey from behind the glass doors of the cabinet in the dining room. His father had a beer instead, and if someone had seen them all there, standing around the tiny kitchen trying to stay out of Juan's mom's way, they would've thought they did this kind of thing all the time.

His father leaned against the fridge, holding his beer down around his leg. He was wearing the same jeans and a clean T-shirt. His hair was stuck together a little from sweat.

Juan stared at him from a stool next to Steven's. Once, Juan had said that Steven's mother was hot, for a mom. It had been one of those moments when you think you're on the same page as someone, and it turns out you're not even in the same book.

This was weirder. It didn't matter whose dad he was. They were both looking at a stranger.

His father said he was going to pay to have a notice in the *Times*. Juan's parents seemed impressed.

There was talk of what the papers had said.

Juan's mom asked politely about San Diego. Steven liked her Greek accent. She had a black braid that reached past her butt. She was curvy. Her name was Anna. She made giant paintings of jungles, and wasn't much taller than Steven.

Juan nudged his knee and bent his head slightly in the direction of his room. No one said anything when they got up and left.

Juan's room was really the pantry. It was too small for a twin bed; he slept on a camp cot. When Steven slept over, they folded up the cot and used sleeping bags. Even then, Steven always ended up with his face pressed against the books and toys on the shelves.

Juan closed the door and turned the ceiling fan on high. It sounded like it could come right out of the Sheetrock. They lay on top of their sleeping bags, staring up at the fan going crazy.

"He looks like you," Juan said.

"Yeah," Steven said.

Juan stuck his legs and arms straight up, like he was the letter *U*. "Let's read the letters," he said.

"We did," Steven said. "Me and McGuire."

Juan seemed kind of hurt. "Well?" he said.

"Nothing," Steven said. He thought of the letter from his father. He imagined the guy in the kitchen putting that letter in his mailbox in San Diego. He wondered what his mother had written about. He didn't know his mother had written to his father. He didn't know his father had written back.

"What'd McGuire say?" Juan asked.

"About what?" Steven asked.

Juan looked at him like he was stupid. "About everything," he said.

"I didn't tell him," Steven said.

Juan dropped his legs and sat up. "You didn't tell him? You didn't tell him about what? About anything?"

Steven talked to the ceiling. "I showed him the letters. I told him where we got them."

"Are we in trouble?" Juan asked.

Steven shook his head.

Then Juan said, "That's it? What did you talk about for so long?"

Steven tried to shrug lying down. It came out like a twitch.

"Why?" Juan asked, not even trying to keep how totally baffled he was out of his voice. "Why?" he asked again, more quietly.

"Because," Steven said. He had no idea how to finish the sentence.

"Are you trying to figure things out for yourself?" Juan asked. "Do you not trust McGuire?" He threw some more theories out. None of them seemed right.

"I don't know," Steven said.

"You're saying that a lot," he said. He wasn't being mean.

"I know," Steven said.

They were quiet. Something clanged in the kitchen.

Juan said, "You gotta tell someone about Manuel and the guy."

"I know," Steven said.

Juan said, "The guy is, like, *after* you."

"Maybe," Steven said.

"*I* should tell someone," Juan said.

Steven felt bad that he was making Juan feel bad. "I'll tell him," he said. "I just want to think a little more. I keep feeling like there's some little thing I'm forgetting."

Juan didn't look convinced; he looked sympathetic.

"Maybe your dad could help," he said. "I mean, if there's something about McGuire you don't like."

They lay there. It was like their own little sweatbox.

"He seems okay," Juan said.

Steven didn't say anything.

"San Diego could be okay," Juan said.

He said it like he wasn't just saying it to be nice or make Steven feel better.

Steven stared at the fan. He picked a blade and counted its revolutions. "Would you think it was fucked up if I felt worse about leaving here than about my mom?" he asked.

Juan moved his arms and legs like he was making snow angels. He said, "Sometimes fucked up's just the play of the day."

Someone knocked.

"Yes?" Juan said in his little old lady voice. "Who is it?"

"Uh, it's me . . . Steven's father." He cleared his throat.

"We know who you are," Juan said. "Enter!"

The door opened. Juan had to pull his legs up.

"Listen," Steven's father said. "Anna just told me about the card." He knelt down by Steven's head. "Are you all right?"

Steven nodded.

"What did Detective McGuire say?" he asked.

"He said the lab was going to look at it," Steven said.

"Did he have any theories?" his father asked.

"I don't know," Steven said. He looked at Juan.

"What do you mean? Nothing? He had nothing to say about this? Did he say you're in danger? Did he say there was anything we could do?" He was getting worked up. He stopped himself, took a breath. "Sorry." He put a hand out like Steven was the one who needed calming down. "Don't worry," he said. "I'll talk to him about it."

Steven told him about the uniform guy.

"So, listen," he said, "I think we better think about San Diego sooner than we planned. You could start the school year on time."

School, Steven thought. "Last year," he said, "we made a replica of a Colonial house."

His dad and Juan didn't say anything. The fan was right over his father's head, like he was wearing some lunatic beanie.

"I was in charge of the chimney. I collected rocks from the park. We didn't use any glue. We raised the walls with tiny ropes." He didn't know why he was telling them about this, but it felt good to do it. "It was cool," he said.

"Sounds cool," his father said. He sounded like he meant it. He stood. "Okay," he said. "So let's think about that earlier departure." He nudged Steven's foot with his own, and then he just stood there. For minutes.

"What're you doing?" Juan asked.

His father took them both in. "Nothing," he said.

"Wanna sit down?" Juan asked.

He folded his long legs under him like a horse and balanced his beer on his thigh, and they sat there like that until Anna called them for dinner.

five

Some days, he spent whole hours with her in his head.
Most days, he didn't.

McGuire said they were free to go through the apartment.
His father said they were leaving for San Diego in a week and
complained about how long everything took in the city, about the
lab turning up nothing on the notes Steven had gotten. Steven said
he wanted to go through the apartment by himself at first. When
he was ready, he'd let whoever come in with boxes and trash bags.

The second note was slipped under the apartment door. It
hadn't been there when Steven arrived. It was there when he left.
Same small envelope. No picture this time. Just a plain white
card, same block letters. "I can't tell you my name. I'm sorry. Are
you taking care of yourself?"

The third one was in his mother's locker at the hospital the day
he went to go through that stuff. He almost missed it.

It was a postcard of San Diego's skyline. It said *San Diego* in happy script across the front. On the back was written, "All the best for your new life."

He knew he should've been scared. He felt the way you feel when you get picked out of the audience to help with the show. The notes meant the guy must know him. He'd met a lot of the guys his mother knew. A lot of them had liked pretending they knew him better than they did.

He didn't tell anyone. He folded them into quarters and put them in his shoe. Their hard edges poked him through his socks. At the end of the day, they were flattened and damp, and he moved them to the waistband of his underwear, worrying their edges and folds with his fingers until he fell asleep.

the uniform guy didn't talk much. Steven didn't take it personally.

At the funeral, there were two more uniform guys and a couple without uniforms. They stood in the back of the chapel trying to keep out of the way. Everyone knew who they were.

The service was a service. His mother was Catholic, but not a real Catholic, and had no brothers or sisters, and her parents were both dead, and his father was Jewish. The cops were the only interesting thing about the whole afternoon. Even the reporters had lost interest by then. Apparently, the longer a case went unsolved, the bigger the chance that it would never be solved. McGuire had said, "Generally, age is not good for a case." A *luncher,* the cops called it. As in "We may end up eating this one." He was learning all sorts of things.

Phil had been trying all week to see him alone. At the service, every time he headed toward Steven, one of the cops angled him off. When Phil caught his eye, Steven acted like he had nothing to say about anything. But Phil wasn't stupid. He knew he was being treated like one of the bad guys.

There were people Steven knew and people he didn't. No one wearing jeans, a white T-shirt, and green and white Adidas.

The kids from school sat in a knot at the back. His teachers were there, and the principal. A woman he didn't recognize stared at him, crying. Christine kept catching his eye and blowing him kisses. Mrs. Carpanetti was there, in black with a black scarf on her head. Michael wasn't. Steven wasn't surprised. Michael wasn't into things like this. Manuel and Tina and the girls came in a few minutes late. Manuel gave him a little wave.

Juan and his mom and dad were in his row. His father sat on his other side. People looked at the two of them. He hoped they looked good together. Natural.

His father was wearing a black suit and a white shirt. He'd forgotten to bring a tie. He'd called and asked if Steven thought he should buy one. Steven had been surprised.

It was a closed coffin, and Steven had said no when the funeral director guy had asked if he wanted to see her before the service began. In the morgue, she'd been on a table in a refrigerated vault. Her head had been propped up on a black rubber block.

He'd said no when his father asked if he wanted to speak. No about having a party afterward.

He sat there on the hard chair in the suit his father had bought for him and imagined saying no to what he could, yes to what he had to. That's how his life would go.

The priest's mouth moved. Steven scanned faces and heads, thinking: You? You?

His father nudged him and mouthed, "Okay?"

Steven nodded.

She said he was the slowest boy in the world. She said he'd forget to put on clothes if she wasn't there to remind him. You should just get down on your knees and thank God for me, she said.

The day before she died, they were wrestling on her bed. He was wet from the shower, and she said by the time he got his jammies on, she'd be an old lady. He pulled back hard to get out of her grip, misjudged the edge of the bed, and put his knee down on air. She grabbed his arm. His head stopped inches from the floor. They were like those ice skaters from the Olympics.

He turned away from his father a little, shielded his arm with his body, and pushed his sleeve up enough. The bruise was the size of her thumb, small and oval. Every day he made sure it was still there.

"What're you doing?" his father whispered.

"Nothing," he said, letting his sleeve fall.

His father moved in closer, tucking Steven under his arm. He didn't seem like the person his mother had described. He didn't seem like just some rich guy. If his mother had liked his father more, it might've made everything easier now.

It wasn't hard to find Manuel after the service. Tina kept hugging Steven, then pulling back, holding his shoulders, looking at him and crying. She hung on him; her girls hung on her, one to each leg. They were some kind of giant puppet, some extinct animal.

"Tina," Manuel said, putting a hand on her shoulder, "give the boy some air."

She shrugged his hand off. "I'll give you some air," she said without any crabbiness at all.

He sighed and reached down to the girls. "Come," he said. "Let your mother alone." He took the girls across the room to the flower arrangements by the front door.

Tina leaned in close. "Your neighbors," she said. "My door doesn't stop ringing with people wanting to know business that isn't theirs."

Manuel was pointing to flowers and the girls were announcing the colors. His back was to Steven.

His father was next to Manuel, waving Steven over. Steven could see the black limo out the open door behind his father. He wondered if he could ask for Manuel to ride with them.

His father and Manuel started talking. When had they met? The girls played hide-and-seek behind the men's legs.

Could it have been his father in the apartment? He tried to hear the voice for the nine-hundreth time. "I owe you." "I owe you." He watched his father's mouth and laid the line over what he was seeing.

"Mrs. Carpanetti," Tina said. "She's the only human being in the whole building. She asked about you, and nothing else."

A reporter, Steven thought. Could it have been a reporter? He didn't think Manuel would've let a reporter in.

Manuel was nodding and looking at his feet. It was weird to see him in something other than work shoes. He was acting the way he acted around people he worked for.

Juan came over. "The car's ready," he said. "Your dad said to get you."

"I need to talk to Manuel," Steven said.

"My Manuel?" Tina asked.

"Here?" Juan said.

Steven asked Tina if she'd mind telling his father that he needed a minute, and asking Manuel if he'd come over.

She looked a little surprised, and a little like she was about to smile, but she said, "Sure," and headed over to the two men.

Juan said, "What're you thinking?"

"I need to know who was in the apartment," Steven said.

"I know," he said. "But now? Here?"

The three grown-ups were talking. His father checked his watch. Manuel looked over. Steven tried to make his face look kind.

Juan swung Steven's arm a little. "Are you okay?"

Everyone was worried. Everyone had been watching him for warning signs, danger signals. First, they'd been worried he'd be feeling too much. Then, not enough.

His father was walking out to the limo driver. Tina was rounding up the girls. Manuel was heading Steven's way.

"One thing about my mother dying," Steven said. "It's a whole lot easier to get my way."

"Steven," Juan said. He almost never used Steven's real name.

"I'm okay," Steven said.

He could see Juan deciding to let it go.

"Maybe your life is gonna be better," Juan said. But when he saw Steven's face, he apologized.

they sat in the room they'd just come out of. The coffin was gone. The chairs were lined up as if things were about to begin instead of already over.

Manuel sat the way he sat in the old dining chair he pulled out to the stoop. His expression said: I'm worried.

"Who was with you the other day in the apartment?" Steven asked.

He tried to watch Manuel the way McGuire watched people. He had no idea what he was looking for. There was more worry. He couldn't tell if Manuel was thinking about lying.

"What other day?" he asked.

"I was there," Steven said.

"You were there," he repeated, as if Steven were speaking another language.

He was thinking. "The window," he said.

"Who was it?" Steven asked.

They'd never talked like this with one another. Manuel glanced toward the door. It stayed closed.

"*Hijo,*" he said. It sounded like he was going to say something else, but then he didn't.

He sat up straight. His jacket was an old winter one, too warm and too small. His big wristbones poked out of the sleeves like Frankenstein's. He looked right at Steven. "I was there; you're right. But there wasn't no one with me."

Steven's face, his neck, the top of his head got hot. "You're lying," he said.

Manuel kept his eyes on him and shook his head. "Just me, *hijo.*"

Steven felt five years old. Tears were starting. "So what were you doing there then?" His voice was wrong. "I could tell Detective McGuire," he said.

"You could do that," Manuel said.

"Why're you lying to me?" Steven said.

Manuel looked at the space where the coffin had been. He rubbed his kneecaps with the heels of his hands.

"I'm sorry," he said.

"You don't lie to me," Steven said. He'd meant it to sound fierce. It came out something else. More tears. His stomach again. "You like me."

Manuel nodded. "I do," he said.

Steven couldn't stop crying. He hit his cheek with an open hand. He did it again.

Manuel reached over and held his wrist. "No, no, no, no, no," he said. He sounded like a train.

"I can't tell you nothing," he said. "But you gotta trust me. It wasn't no one did those things to your mama."

Manuel's big brown hand was around his own skinny wrist.

He put his other hand on the back of Steven's neck and pulled him in. The top of Steven's head butted him in the chest. He smelled of his little girls and the lobby. Steven looked at the floor between their feet. The door opened. Steven could hear the sounds of the front hall clearing out.

"Don't go," he said.

"No, man," Manuel said, his hand rocking Steven's neck. "For sure, I won't."

his father said that Steven needed to "talk to someone." Steven figured getting through an hour with anyone would be easier than arguing with a father he didn't know at all.

After, he told his father that the lady had been good. He wasn't lying, but he knew he wasn't going to tell her about what Manuel had said, and if he wasn't going to talk about that, he didn't see the point of talking at all. He told his father that he didn't want to see her again.

His father asked him to think about it.

He said he would.

the week after the funeral, a couple of days before they were leaving, McGuire called off the uniform guy. "No more notes," he said. "Seems like our guy's gonna leave you outta all this."

Tell him about Manuel, Steven thought. But he didn't.

"Let's go get some weed," Juan said. It was like he'd been trying really hard to be good while they focused on more important stuff, but now that the uniform guy was gone, it was permission to be normal again. They'd gotten stoned twice. But it was normal to act like they did it all the time.

They went to the head shop on Columbus. It was between two brick buildings, a narrow alley with a door and a roof. A small Indian woman sat at the back end of it, unable to push her chair more than a few inches from the end table she used as a desk. She used a watch calculator to save space. The walls were lined with sheets of pegboard. Feather and bead earrings, bracelets, and necklaces hung from metal hooks. Cellophane packages of incense. Dark brown bottles of oils and stuff. Scarves and hats hung on clothespins from the ceiling. Nickel and dime bags of pot in small manila envelopes. Everything was small. It was like shopping for drugs in a dollhouse.

They went to Central Park, one of those little gazebo things by the pond. There was Burger King stuff on the bench that someone had just left there, and a crumpled condom in the corner.

They sat on the edge of the railing, their backs to the path. The feeling of being stoned was good. The feeling about being stoned wasn't. Nothing could get rid of the weirdness in his stomach.

"It could be Manuel," Juan said, like he knew Steven didn't want to hear it.

The sky was the color of sour milk. The backs of his thighs were sweating. Everything smelled worse in the heat.

"He liked her," Steven said. He'd started thinking about her in the past tense. Just in the last day. "He likes me," he said.

"He *lied* to you," Juan said.

"I know," Steven said. "I was there."

"So why'd he lie?" Juan asked, again.

"Why'd he lie?" Steven repeated, as if repeating it enough would make an answer appear.

"He didn't really lie," Steven said. "He didn't tell the whole truth."

Juan was quiet.

They heard tiny bells behind them. It was the Cat Man, an old black man dressed in layers of beige clothes who circled the park pulling a haphazard train of little red wagons, tricycles, toddlers' bikes with training wheels, and a shopping cart behind him. On every handlebar, seat, and basket, a cat. Some with one eye. Some with three legs. One with eight toes. The Cat Man rang finger-bells, clanged tiny cymbals, hit small metal wind chimes, a one-man concert for his cats.

They watched him make his slow way down the path and out of sight.

"You gotta tell someone," Juan said.

"Okay," Steven said.

"People don't really like people they work for," Juan said.

"He liked us," Steven said again.

"Who liked you?" Phil asked from the path.

Juan glanced at Steven. Steven could tell he was thinking: I can outrun him. Steven didn't think he could. His hand was in his pocket. He closed it around the damp manila envelope.

Phil ducked into the gazebo and sat on the bench across from them. He looked out at the pond. Some guy was rowing a girl and a baby around. He didn't look so happy.

Tell him about Manuel, Steven thought.

Phil moved his feet inches one way, then inches the other. He asked how he'd been.

Steven shrugged. "Good," he said. It felt like he was keeping everything from everyone.

Phil didn't seem to have heard. "Listen," he said to Juan. "I need to talk to Steven. He'll meet you at home."

Juan looked skeptical. "We're supposed to hang out together," he said.

"He'll be fine," Phil said. He didn't sound like a murderer.

"I'll wait," Juan said, pointing at a bench up on the path.

Phil shrugged, and Juan left. He didn't sit on the bench; he walked around it, keeping an eye on them.

"They think I did it," Phil said.

Steven didn't say anything. Some of the leaves behind the

gazebo were already yellow and orange. There were years ahead of him without her.

"Do you?" Phil asked.

"No," Steven said. He could feel his heart, but he didn't know if that was because he believed himself or because he didn't.

He waited for Phil to tell him he hadn't.

Phil swept the Burger King stuff off the bench and out the back end of the gazebo with his forearm. Steven watched the cup of soda spill and roll down the short hill to the mud at the edge of the pond.

"I loved your mom," Phil said. He waited.

"Yeah," Steven said.

"Think she loved me?" he asked.

Steven still thought of him as his teacher. Phil used to bring green peppers to school for his lunch. He ate them whole, like an apple. It was weird to have this conversation with him. "I don't know how to tell those kinds of things," he said.

One time his mother had made him sit in a field of daffodils at the base of Belvedere Castle.

Phil looked sad. "She talked about you a lot," Steven said.

Juan was perched on the back of the bench, watching. Steven waved. Juan still looked worried.

"She talked about you a lot," Phil said.

It made Steven feel better. He couldn't believe it did that.

An old man and an old woman rowed by. He didn't look strong enough to row them anywhere. They looked like brother and sister. His face said: There isn't anywhere I'd rather be.

"Who do you think did it?" Steven asked, still watching the old couple.

He could feel Phil's eyes on him.

"There was another man," Phil said.

"I know," Steven said. There were a lot of other men, he thought.

"We argued about him," Phil said.

"I know," Steven said.

"Did you meet him?" Phil asked.

"I don't know," Steven said. The old woman tilted her head back to the sun.

"There was someone named Kurt," Steven said.

Phil was quiet, then he said, "I didn't know a Kurt."

Steven saw his mother with her feet in Kurt's lap, and he was glad Phil didn't have that picture in his mind.

"Could you do something for me?" Steven asked.

Phil was surprised.

"Could you say, 'I owe you'?"

Phil was confused. He didn't say anything.

"There was someone in the apartment the other day," Steven said. "Manuel and someone else. A guy."

"How do you know?" Phil asked.

Steven explained.

"It wasn't me," he said.

"I know," Steven said.

They stared at one another.

"So, can you say it?" Steven asked.

He said it and looked at Steven. "Well?" he asked.

It didn't help one way or the other. "I don't know," Steven said.

"It wasn't me," Phil said again.

"Okay," Steven said.

The old couple were laughing. Phil glanced over his shoulder at them. "I don't think they're gonna catch the guy," he said.

Tell him about Manuel lying, Steven thought. Why aren't you telling him about that?

"Me neither," Steven said. Time was passing. People had other things to think about. Or they didn't have enough interest in this. In them. He didn't want to be responsible for making people care again, or still. Maybe that's why he wasn't saying anything about Manuel.

He was feeling sorry for himself. His mother hated it when he did that.

"What's gonna happen to me?" he said.

Phil looked at him like he was pulling away on a bus. "Oh, bud," he said. "You'll move to San Diego and live with your dad and your sister and brother. And things will be hard, and then things'll get easier."

"And stepmom," Steven said. "I have a stepmom."

Phil nodded.

"She doesn't want me. She and my dad have like a contract about it," Steven said.

"You can't take that personally," Phil said. "She doesn't even know you. When she gets to know you, she won't feel that way anymore. She'll be ashamed she ever felt that way."

"I can take it personally," Steven said.

They sat there.

"Do you think catching the guy would make me feel better?" Steven asked.

Phil didn't answer. He seemed to be considering the question. Steven could be having this conversation with the guy who'd killed his mother. He needed Phil not to be the guy.

"You'll always miss your mom," Phil said.

It was true. Whether they caught the guy or not, whether his stepmother ever came to like him, whether his father turned out to be someone he admired, whether he turned out to be someone he liked. The one thing he could see in the open space ahead of him was the missing shape of his mother. It was reassuring to know it would always be there. He folded her in half, in quarters. He swallowed her. She would stay there, slowly unfolding for the rest of his life.

II

December 1977

six

Lily Chin didn't like Christmas shopping. It embarrassed her to walk up Madison laden with bags of unnecessary objects from Nikolai's favorite stores. When the doorman opened the glass doors to Nikolai's building, reaching to relieve her of her purchases, she felt like crying. She registered the extremity of the reaction.

"Whadja get for me?" a vaguely southern voice from behind her asked, and something slipped from her throat to her chest. Matthew Cullen was leaning against a parked car. He wore a tweed jacket with the collar turned up and a black scarf, and squinted at her. He remained good-looking. "Don't I know you?" he asked.

They hadn't seen each other in four years.

The doorman hovered, unsure whether to step in.

Lily stilled her face. "You used to," she said, in a voice that she hoped held no sense of invitation.

He held a palm to his chest, swaying as if struck. His gestures had always been like that.

The doorman held the door wider, but when she didn't go through it, he let it swing closed, moving a discrete distance away into the depths of the lobby.

Matthew glanced up at the building. "I hear you're getting married," he said.

He'd always had the ability to make her feel as if she were the setup for jokes she didn't get. She had never asked how he knew the things he knew about her. She had merely sunned herself in the warmth of the knowledge. It had been, for a while, the best intimacy she had known.

"What do you want?" she asked, not unkindly.

He smiled. "There's my Lily," he said. "Beautiful, brisk Lily."

She had an image of his naked body in Nikolai's bed. His body had been imperfect in perfect ways. She took a breath. Her chest was closed, the air reaching her lungs thin and tight.

"It's lovely to see you," she said, gathering her packages.

The doorman had the door open, pretending, in that doorman way, not to see.

Matthew leaned in close and said quietly into her collar, "What have I ever wanted?" She could feel his breath through her scarf.

He waited, and then stuffed his hands into his jeans pockets, and left.

The doorman took her packages, and as she slipped through the front door she managed a thank-you, avoiding his eyes.

Nikolai, Nikolai, Nikolai, she thought, to bring her back to this life. This wasn't just the building Nikolai lived in; this was Nikolai's Building, as in a building Nikolai owned. He owned many.

They would be hers, too, he liked to say, kissing her on the nose.

She did not feel the entrepreneurial glee that she understood he wished for her to feel when he said things like that, that he himself felt when thinking of real estate. Real estate for him was what education had been for her immigrant parents. What pornography was for others.

They were to be married in two months, on Valentine's Day. His idea. At the Plaza. Also his idea. Everything else was up to her. He trusted her completely. This announcement had had the effect of draining her of her usual confidence in matters of logistics, and she'd spent the last month second-guessing herself and checking everything with him. She did this during meals, riding around the city in his Town Car, during their lovemaking.

Don't worry, he would say, kissing her eyelids or tracing a line down the center of her body as if following a road on a map. What you want is what I want.

But he wanted too many things that she could do without. Horse-drawn carriages, champagne fountains, ice sculptures in the shape of his buildings, heralds blowing horns.

"Crossing things off your lists?" the doorman asked, smiling.

Even her boyfriend's doormen knew she liked lists.

"Trying," she said. "It's hard," she added, and then was ashamed for saying it. Whatever was hard in her life was harder in his.

He pushed the elevator button and stood waiting with her. She concentrated on remembering something about him. Nikolai knew the full names of everyone who worked in the building. He knew details about their lives: wives, children, favorite teams. At Christmas, he labeled the holiday envelopes without consulting the list the board sent around.

I'm one of you, she wanted to say. Her father was a bus driver. Her mother was a seamstress. She didn't live in a place like this.

She lived on 102nd between Riverside and West End in a studio. And made the most of what she had. Her rent was probably less than his.

Manuel. This one's name was Manuel. The one, she was fairly certain, Nikolai had known for several years, the one he'd gotten this job for. She tried to think of something else, and came up with nothing but: *Don't tell Nikolai about Matthew.* Their reflections morphed in the dull gold of the doors.

The elevator came, and he held the door with his foot to let her pass, arranged her packages around her, and reached in to press three. All these things would've been easier for her to do.

"Have a nice night, Ms. Chin," he said.

Oh, yes, she thought. The one who had that way of saying her name. His accent and inflection made her name sound like a gangster's nickname. Lily the Chin. Or maybe like what she was: a preschool teacher.

She tried to remember where he was from. Somewhere Caribbean. Somewhere south and warm. The specifics evaded her.

"Thank you, Manuel," she said. "You too, Manuel."

It was only four o'clock but the apartment was already darkening. She slipped off her boots and padded around, turning on lights. All the lights, even in rooms she had no intention of inhabiting. She did this anytime she came here. At her parents' apartment in Queens, there were never any lights on. She'd come home from school, and the table would be set for dinner in a dark kitchen; her mother and father would be waiting for her, looking at each other across a dark living room. When she turned on the lights, they winced.

She wandered the apartment, a balloon trying to find its way back to earth. This will be my living room, she thought. This will be my study. My guest room for my guests. My bathrooms. There were four bedrooms, each with its own bath. It was like a hotel. When she confided to Nikolai that none of it felt like hers, he said not to worry, this was their Trainer Apartment; they shouldn't get too attached. He was grim about being on only the third floor. It bothered him to be eye-level with the trees. In his mind he had them in the penthouse of a building he hadn't yet bought.

She was twenty-eight. She had an undergraduate degree in English from Barnard and a master's in education from Teacher's College. She'd grown up in Flushing, Queens, the only child of Harry and Priscilla Chin. Those were not their birth names, but when they'd come to this country fleeing the Communists, they'd taken American names and never looked back. They spoke broken English to each other even when they were alone. They found her high school interest in China and things Chinese baffling and a little alarming, something to keep an eye on, like a tick bite.

Now their neighborhood was Chinese, but then it had been Koreatown, the streets lined with the telltale vertical store signs. Their Korean neighbors in Flushing regarded the Chinese Chins with a wary eye. Everyone else assumed they were Korean. Walking home from school, she smelled kim chi and one particular brand of Korean incense.

College and graduate school had been happy places for her. It was as if someone had taken her into a clean building, opened a

door onto a tastefully furnished room with a well-stocked refrig-
erator, and said, "Stay as long as you like."

She'd found her professors intelligent if not always interesting,
and her peers neither, but inoffensive, for the most part, and willing to let her be. For the first year, she'd lived at home, twice a
day riding what the regulars called the International Express, the
number seven from Manhattan to Queens, which passed through
some of the most ethnically diverse neighborhoods around: Sun-
nyside, Woodside, Jackson Heights, Elmhurst, Corona, ending at
Main Street, Flushing.

She'd had the same roommate for the next three years, an
earnest and enthusiastic softball player from Minnesota, whom
she hadn't spoken to since, a situation about which neither of
them harbored ill feelings.

Her senior year, she slept with a tall, shy boy from Nebraska
the week before he left to join his father's insurance company in
Omaha. He was blond and Nordic and she'd been neither pleased
nor traumatized by their quiet lovemaking. She was glad to have
her virginity behind her, but had no energy to pursue further
lovers.

Matthew Cullen had been a friend of a friend of a friend, whom
she'd met the one and only time her fellow graduate students had
been able to convince her to go out with them. A good-looking per-
petual Columbia student with a soft southern accent. She thought at
first that she'd met him before, but there'd been dozens of boys like
him at school, southern trust-fund boys going to the proper north-
eastern colleges, always on the verge of getting kicked out, buoyed
by the luxury of the family oil or tobacco business as safety net.

He, however, had kissed her hand, said, "How'd the picnic

go?", enjoyed her confusion, and then reminded her that he'd flirted with her a year or so back. She'd been walking down 102nd street, carrying a bowl of something, on her way to the park.

"Flirted?" Lily had said, and he had laughed, remarking that it was true, sometimes what he intended to communicate wasn't all that clear.

Her knowledge of and vague contempt for his type were not enough to tamper with the feelings he inspired. He was the good-natured dog she had wanted and been forbidden as a child. The one who tilts his eyebrows at you, letting you know that all he wants in the world is your hand on his head. She had more to drink than she usually did. She smoked a joint for the first and last time in her life. But when they closed the door to her apartment behind them, her head was not spinning. She was, to her considerable surprise, in perfect control of her desires and the behaviors they elicited.

Everything about him said: *If you come to me, I will save you,* and so for months she had gone to him, and gone to him, feeling taken care of in ways that suggested she might never touch the earth again.

And then he had betrayed her with someone about whom Lily knew almost nothing. She had called Lily, and Lily had been reminded of what she had, of course, known all along: asking someone to save you was the same thing as asking for a certain kind of destruction. His genuine sadness about his own behavior did not temper the damage, though it had taken all she had to tell him to leave, to refuse the phone calls, to deny the ache of missing them when they stopped.

And so he returned to her often. The crisp citrus smell of his cheek, the thick denim of his jeans against the cotton of her underwear, his hand on her hip like a hinge. The way he would say, "I know what you're thinking," and be right. The version of herself he had revealed, from which she'd chosen to look away.

She'd put herself back on track. Teacher's College for graduate school, an apartment within walking distance, and then a job working at a private preschool in the same neighborhood.

She trusted people until they gave her enough reasons not to. This was a useful trait in the face of two- and three-year-olds and their parents, the liberal white pioneers of the Upper West Side. The children had liked her instantly, tumbling and fizzing around her like bubbles up the sides of a still glass. The parents had not, at least not instantly, watching their children's enthusiasm for this quiet woman with confusion and a small sense of betrayal. There was only one parent whom Lily herself didn't like. Sally Grossman. Sometimes she'd turned the name over in her mouth. Sally's daughter, Ruth, was a blond girl with a round head and Who-from-Whoville blue eyes who had started last fall. Ruth had spina bifida. When they'd interviewed, Sally had closed the interview by saying, "She won't be any trouble. She can't walk." And Lily had decided she disliked Sally Grossman. And it was hard, once Lily had made up her mind about something, to find a way to change it.

On days when she'd had to talk with Sally more than she liked to, she allowed herself a beer at the bar a few blocks away from school. She'd gone there once or twice as a student and felt, falsely, she knew, comfortable walking in there alone. She always sat at the corner of the bar nearest the bartender, just as she always sat in the conductor's car on the subway. Living alone, she'd learned some tricks: Put a pair of construction boots outside the door. Next to them, a big dog chain and a water bowl. New York could be perfectly safe if you lived by certain rules and took certain precautions. Since the murder on her block the summer before last, this had been a harder belief in which to maintain faith. Of course, there were murders all the time in New York, but not all of them were two houses down, and not all of the victims had a child in the upper grades of Lily's school.

That woman, she'd decided, based on no real knowledge, must not have had clear enough rules, or must not have stuck to them well enough. After that there'd been the Son of Sam killings, and the blackout rioting and arson, and she'd had to work hard to resist feeling as if the woman's murder had been the beginning of some kind of horrible slide.

One day in September, more than a year after the murder two houses down, someone had spoken to her while she sat on her stool, in her corner.

It was Nikolai, though he introduced himself as Nick. Nick Belov, he said, and because of his odd mix of Russian and New York accents, Lily thought she heard *Belove*, like some archaic form of *Beloved*. She would learn that his accent came and went depending on the audience. The longer he spoke with you, the more he sounded like you.

He was a big man, older than she by ten or fifteen years. His brown hair was layered and already graying. It brushed his shoulders like a feather duster. Everything about him was oversized: his nose, his chin, his cheekbones. He gestured as if on a second-story balcony overlooking a grand piazza filled with thousands of his people. His eyes were olive green and they swept the room as if on lookout. Behind the movement, she imagined a vast sadness.

That night he wore a beige dress shirt with French cuffs and cuff links with a crest that featured crossed swords. His pants were dark brown and speckled with small stains. He'd saved money on his shoes. He gesticulated so dramatically with his right hand that it took Lily a moment to realize that he was missing the index finger from his left.

"Oh," she exclaimed, surprising herself by reaching out and touching the wrinkled nub of the joint.

He didn't pull away. He took her finger and pressed it gently but firmly around the place where his finger should've been. The topographical maps of elementary school came back to her.

"The price I paid for the rudeness of pointing," he said.

She had no idea what he could mean.

He told her about the orphanage in Russia where he had been raised after his parents died, murdered by robbers when he was six. "You can't imagine," he said, waving his good hand. "Think worse than Dickens," he said.

"Gogol," she said, pulling the name from the World Literature class she'd taken at school.

"On your nose," he said, putting a finger to her nose, and she felt the first warmth of getting something right with him.

He was nothing like she was but familiar nonetheless. She wouldn't have been surprised to learn that even in her neighborhood, where you had to walk for blocks before seeing a white person, he'd watched her play her childhood games on her stoop from his across the street.

Later, he'd revealed that he'd seen her at the bar before, and

she'd understood why he'd seemed so familiar, and she'd felt a little silly and told herself, as she often did, to remember that there
were usually logical explanations for all those illogical feelings that
wouldn't quite be placed.

"I watched you many times," he told her. "Always so sad, so
pinched." He made a fist and held it over his heart. "I think in my
head, such a beautiful girl."

And then she didn't feel silly. Hearing him describe her sadness made her think again that *he* was sad. She saw it as the still
surface of a frozen lake, and she wanted to put on the ice skates
she hadn't worn since her lessons as a child and pirouette
through its hardness.

He'd worked his way through Columbia undergrad as a dish-
washer in the dining halls, and had continued there for one semes-
ter of business school before losing patience with the pace. He'd
made investors out of his classmates and professors, selling them
on the opportunity of state-sponsored middle-income co-ops and
tax-abatement programs. His first building was a seven-story
apartment house in Brooklyn Heights that he sold three years after
buying it for five times what he'd paid. "The rest," he'd said,
sweeping his arm around as if he now owned all that she could see,
"is history."

She was charmed by his use of clichés. She liked that he'd liked
the bar for the same reasons she had. It seemed friendly without
being pretentious. He seemed as different from Matthew as possible, yet there was something familiar about the feelings the two
men inspired in her, and that, she decided, was a good thing. So
when he asked her if he could walk her home, she said yes, as if
saying yes were something she did all the time.

100 · karen shepard

They walked down Broadway to 107th. They veered west and walked down West End to 102nd. They crossed West End. She could see her building halfway down the block. She said, "You don't have to walk me all the way," and he looked at her and threw his head back, laughing his big laugh. "You kill me," he said.

He put his arm around her and squeezed her to his side. She imagined herself as Eve in reverse. A woman burrowing her way between Adam's ribs, nestling there as if returning home.

She had to admit now that it embarrassed her to have to say that she and her fiancé had met at a bar. His friends liked to tease her about it, raising their eyebrows and making their animal sounds. Her parents adored him, thrilled that he'd proposed after such a short time, though in the four months he'd been with her, he'd probably said no more than fifty words to them. It was as if they'd convinced him that they didn't speak English. She could tell they adored him by how they talked about him in the third person. "Look. He seems tired." "Look. He's watching TV." "Look. He's eating." Even when they spoke English, he acted as if they weren't.

She hid the new purchases in the back of what would be her study closet. Nikolai never went in there. He'd already encouraged her to use the room as a study. "You spend so much time over here, you might as well get going on making it your place," he'd said, passing her his credit card.

She knew that her apartment was a place he only liked to visit. "Lily's Strange and Wondrous World," he called it. He said her ability to pull together thrift store purchases made the Park Avenue ladies feel generic in terms of their style sense. It seemed to her that the Park Avenue ladies felt about her something very different from the feelings he described.

In February, she would be a Park Avenue lady. He was not a Park Avenue man, but wore the accessories as if they'd been tailored for him.

He'd tried to persuade her to leave her job in the middle of the year. He said it wasn't all that different from leaving at the end. "You're easily replaced," he said, not meaning to be insulting. She'd held her ground, and as the wedding grew closer, she was glad. Her days at school were like a sturdy handrail on a steep and unfamiliar set of stairs.

She went to the kitchen to make tea, to loosen the grip seeing Matthew had placed around her chest, to pass the hours before Nikolai would be home, and with him the safety he offered. When she heard his key in the door, the tightness would seep away, and she would close her eyes so they could open to the sight of him walking to her. She hadn't known that feelings like this would be part of a life like hers.

A high school English teacher had made them all write ten-year predictions for themselves before they graduated. Last spring, at the tenth reunion, the teacher had spread them all out. Lily hadn't gone, and when she'd heard about the predictions from the one friend who hadn't let her quietly slip away, she'd been reassured about her own wisdom. The teacher had mailed Lily's predictions to her with a note that said, "Thought you might want these."

Lily had predicted that she would have gone to graduate school in early childhood development, that she'd be teaching at the job she'd had since finishing graduate school. That she'd be unmarried, without children.

Her accuracy had pleased her. It was a good and useful trait—accurate knowledge of oneself. Her relationship with Matthew had been a bump on her life's road, and when thought of that way, as predictable as any other part of her life, it was a source of reassurance rather than anxiety.

The appearance of Nikolai in her life had made her feel as if she had been set down on a rolling sea and told to stand up straight. For a month or two, she'd resisted, but then he had made love to her, and then he had proposed, and instead of trying to stand, she'd let herself float, feeling the delicious lick of waves, imagining a wholly different kind of life. A wholly different kind of woman to inhabit that life.

"I make you a better person," Nikolai liked to whisper during their lovemaking.

Sometimes, just that could bring her to the edge of orgasm.

The service doorbell rang.

She made her way through the kitchen and checked the peephole. A small woman, brown-skinned, thick black hair slicked and twisted into impossible shapes. Multiple hoops hanging from multiple ear piercings. Gold-plated necklaces of various lengths hanging as a shield across the small woman's chest. The woman had no coat. Her dress was wool, tight-fitting. She was wearing black stockings and the wrong kind of shoes. Lily recognized that she was already beginning to think of herself as better than women like this.

She blushed and felt like an impostor. Since Nikolai's proposal, this sensation washed over her occasionally. She hadn't told him, though it was a sensation she knew he'd find familiar. She had once overheard him answer a friend's "How's it going?" with, "You make it through the day without anyone finding out you are a fraud." He had shrugged and stuck out his lower lip. "It's a life."

She collected herself, straightened her sweater, put her house shoes on. I belong, she thought. Right here, opening this door.

"Yes?" she asked, trying to seem kind and curious, but not too curious.

The woman took Lily in, as if checking that she had the right apartment.

"Perhaps you're looking for my fiancé," Lily said. "He's not back from work yet."

The woman shook her head. "I know who he is. I'm looking for you."

Under different circumstances, Lily would've admired her no-nonsense quality. They stood there.

Lily stepped back. "I'm sorry. Come in. Please." She peered at the woman's necklaces. One of them said *Tina* in gold script. "I'm Lily Chin," she said, offering a hand. "And you are . . ." She leaned forward, squinting a little, hating herself as she did it. "Tina?"

Tina shook Lily's hand. She smelled a little of a bakery. "Tina Hernandez," she said.

She didn't want anything to drink. She didn't glance around the apartment. She sat on the edge of the black leather armchair in the living room, her toes turned in, her hands over her knees.

"So," she said. "You don't know me from nobody, so if I told you not to marry Nikolai you wouldn't listen, right?" She looked at Lily. "You look good," she said.

"Thank you," Lily answered, feeling as if anything could happen. Perhaps part of this new life would be strange visits from strange women.

"So Nikolai's your first boyfriend, right?"

Lily took a breath. "I don't mean to be rude, but who are you?" she asked. "How did you get into the building unannounced?"

Tina glanced at her watch, an oversized yellow happy face on a white plastic band that was too big for her wrist. "No one's ever at the service entrance," she said. "He'll be home soon," she added.

Lily waited.

"How do you know that?" she finally asked. Tina didn't answer. Lily reached up and turned off the light.

Tina nodded in the gloom, as if congratulating her on a wise choice.

"Last spring and into this fall, we were together, him and me," she said. "You know: *together*. I'm sorry," she added.

She sat back as if the rest was up to Lily.

This fall, Lily and Nikolai had met. They'd gone to the beach. They'd walked through the park. They'd eaten at the hot dog stand. Was she going to spend her life hearing of her lovers' betrayals?

She asked rational and calm questions, and Tina answered her, and Lily imagined the answers as armor. She imagined dressing herself, piece by piece, her soft white body disappearing behind burnished metal. She would not lose Nikolai as she had lost Matthew.

And then she said, "What is it that you want me to do with this information?"

Tina said, "You can't marry him."

Lily laughed, a short, high bark. She apologized. "Of course I can," she said.

Tina said, "There's something about him. You can't."

Lily looked at her levelly.

"I know, it sounds loco," Tina said. "I can't explain it really. There're things I noticed. Please," she said. "Please."

Lily didn't respond well to this kind of neediness. "Don't be ridiculous," she said. "Things you've noticed?"

"He told me he went to Columbia, but he didn't. He gave my girls notes to give to me."

"Girls?" Lily asked.

Tina looked ashamed and proud. "Two," she said. "Four and a half and two."

"And you have a husband as well?" Lily asked.

"Yes," Tina said, her eyes large and sad. "I'm not perfect," she said, "but that doesn't make me wrong about Nick. We went away for a weekend. Two nights it was supposed to be. In the middle of the first night, I wake up and he's gone. Just gone. I had to get a bus home." She was speaking fast.

Lily had had enough of this. "Maybe he didn't want to be with you anymore," she said.

Tina looked around as if she might find some help in the room. "It's not so much the things he's done as a feeling I have," she said. "I'm good at feelings."

"I'm sure you are," Lily said, standing.

Tina remained sitting. "Please," she said. "Please."

Desperation hung around her, but it was desperation that had nothing to do with Lily, so Lily showed her to the front door and asked her not to contact her again. Tina was still talking as she walked out into the hall. She was still talking when Lily closed the door and swam back to the life she was beginning to feel she deserved.

They made love. They slept. Lily was not someone who believed in insomnia. It was impractical. But here she was at four in the morning, awake.

Nikolai was on his back, his breathing deep and soft. She rolled onto her side, getting close to his profile. At her movement, he reached a hand out and stroked the curve of her hip. She knew he was not awake. He could love her in his sleep. Sometimes he talked to her, and it was only the blankness of his face in the morning that made her understand that he had been sleeping through the entire conversation.

He had never said anything suspicious.

She draped a leg over him and flattened her hand against his sternum. "Nikolai," she whispered. She wondered how quiet she could be and still rouse him. How well was he listening for her in his sleep? "Nikolai," she said again, even softer.

"My treasure," he said, rolling over, his eyes still closed.

"I need to talk with you," she said.

"Okeydokey," he said. He opened his eyes, rubbed them like a toddler, and offered her his face, alert and attentive.

She imagined what she would say. She imagined the impact on his expression.

"Something is wrong?" he asked.

What had she expected? That he would come to her new and virginal? That they would've sprung from the ground, earth's first couple, finding each other across a wide and empty space? She understood that part of why she loved him was because of what her life had been before him. Surely the same logic applied to his feelings. Yet she had told him all about Matthew. What did it matter? What mattered was that he had come to her at all.

She touched his cheek. "Do you love me?"

His expression softened into the opposite of worry. "You crazy girl. You silly chicken." He wound a finger next to his temple. "You are loco," he said, pulling her to him.

She rested her head against his chest. She rose and fell with his breaths. He combed her hair with his fingers and sang her a song she didn't know in Russian.

"Silly goose," she said. "Not chicken. Goose."

What had Matthew ever wanted? Everything. Nothing. And all that lay between.

seven

She stood in her mother's sewing room on a small stool in front of a three-panel mirror. She wore what would be her wedding dress but what right now looked like color and texture without shape. Her mother knelt at her feet, wearing her work clothes. Lily had always thought of them as peasant pajamas. Her lips held a bouquet of pins.

Lily didn't like looking at her mother's head from this angle. And she didn't like looking at her own reflection. She closed her eyes, but felt too dizzy to stay that way. She scanned the room. This had been her bedroom. Her mother had sewed in the corner of the living room by the window until Lily had gone to college. Her mother's Chinese friends had all worked in Manhattan's garment industry, riding the subway with each other and their Dominican coworkers, but Priscilla had insisted on staying at home. Lily remembered marveling at the enormity of what her mother could make in that small space. She'd spend several days hunched over indistinguishable piles of cloth, and then would rise, shaking out a silk pantsuit, a set of Chinese bridesmaid dresses, a pleated skirt with matching collared shirt.

None of this talent had been passed on to Lily. Nothing from her father either, the bus driver with the perfect safety record and the wall full of commendations from the Transit Authority. He knew his passengers' names.

She'd tried taking Driver's Ed once. She'd been too terrified even to touch the wheel, and after several minutes the instructor had squeezed her arm, told her that driving wasn't all it was cracked up to be, and reached across to open her door and release her.

In China, her parents had been physicists.

Sometimes she felt like a character in a fairy tale, the child delivered to the childless couple, never able to fully know or be known.

When her mother had moved into Lily's old room, she'd done so as unobtrusively as possible, leaving as many of Lily's old belongings as she could. Her spelling bee ribbons and awards, her collection of tiny dollhouse food, the Collier's Encyclopedia set they'd paid for in monthly installments, her ice-skating trophies, her class pictures in matching frames that her mother had bought in bulk at the Woolworth's when Lily started kindergarten. Her science fair projects, the poster boards warping and gathering dust. Her father had raided some of them for his own puttering, so they stood there on the shelves, hints of their former selves. Trying to discern the original projects was like identifying a body from dental records.

"Why don't you get rid of all this?" Lily asked.

Her mother's mouth was still full of pins. She shrugged and kept at the hem. Lily had picked the pattern out of a Vogue pattern book. Her mother had wanted to know if Nick liked the dress. Her parents liked saying his name. They said it like they said *America*.

She felt her body warm with anger and resentment. These were impractical feelings she'd banished successfully from her day-to-day life by eliminating their cues. Now, in front of a mirror her father had jerry-rigged from three cheap mirrors that were supposed to be hanging on the backs of hollow doors, above her mother circling her on her knees, Lily was angry. Why didn't her mother do what most seamstresses did—tap her on the calf and make her do the turning? Why did she insist on crawling around like a slave?

Her father was humming in the kitchen, cooking dinner for them. Jiao-tse and something else. Shredded pork and a steamed whole sea bass. It was as if all his talents as a physicist were sublimated into cooking. He had three shelves of cookbooks and tried a different recipe every night. It was the only extravagance they allowed themselves, and Lily stood there thinking of it as pathetic.

"I'm never coming back here," she said.

Her mother sat back on her heels and looked up at her.

"Save this stuff if you want it, but don't think you're saving it for me," she said. She never spoke to her mother like this. She barely spoke to her at all.

Her mother was less pained than baffled. In the kitchen, her father's sounds had quieted. She could tell he was listening.

Her mother put the last pin expertly in Lily's hem. She stood and plucked at the material around Lily's shoulders. Instantly the mass of cloth looked more like a dress.

Lily made a small growl.

Her mother looked at her. Her broad face offered nothing but care. She smoothed her gray hair, tucked a piece back into her bun, as if this gesture alone could set the world straight.

"Why you think we keep all this stuff, crazy girl?" she asked. "Not for you." She thumped her chest with her small, wide hand. "We love you," she said, as if speaking to a deaf child. She tugged expertly at the sleeves of Lily's dress. "You so much smart girl and not know this?"

Lily felt the anger receding, but couldn't figure out how to back out of the situation gracefully. "Well, you should stop thinking about me so much," she said. "You're supposed to think about each other."

Her mother put a hand to her forehead. "*Ai ya,*" she exclaimed, exasperated. "I love him; he love me; we love you. It *why* we love you," she said, enunciating slowly, and Lily had a glimpse of her mother, the physicist, laying out to dimwitted students how the world works.

"Ask Nick," her mother said.

the assistant at the Columbia Student Records Department wasn't being rude, but neither was he being helpful. He had a hawk's nose and a puffed chest, both of which gave him the air of an aristocrat. She almost expected him to speak with a British accent. But his forearms were thick and covered with tattoos: the back of a girl's head, a hammer and shovel, a map of Vietnam. She felt wariness descending on her like a cloak. Sometimes, she'd learned, when you looked Vietnamese it didn't matter that you weren't.

They stood on either side of a Formica counter in a windowless room, and she smiled and told him that she needed to know if a Nikolai Belov had graduated. She wasn't sure of the year. Around 1960, she thought. She stepped back and waited for him to open a drawer and pluck out a file.

He apologized and said he was sorry, but he couldn't give out that information—university policy.

She hadn't planned well enough. She wasn't prepared.

"But I need it," she said.

"Why?" he asked, and she was surprised again and at a loss. Clerks were supposed to grant or deny permission, not ask why.

He was waiting. His eyes were paying such sharp attention that it made her think he was avoiding himself.

"The woman my fiancé used to sleep with has noticed things about him," she said.

He looked as if this was the sort of thing he'd expected. He nodded. "When's the date?" he asked.

"Valentine's Day," she said.

"Four weeks," he said, as if measuring whether that was enough time to get through all that they had to accomplish.

She waited. Nikolai thought she was meeting with the caterer. "I'll come with you," he'd said. "No," she'd insisted, she was working on a surprise for him. "With the caterer?" he'd teased.

She was not good at subterfuge. Now she would have to meet

with the caterer. Now she'd have to come up with a surprise. And still Nikolai would think her behavior odd.

"You look like the Vietnamese prostitute I lost my virginity to," the assistant said.

"I'm Chinese," she said, as if that meant she wasn't allowed to remind him of anyone.

"Do you believe the woman?" he asked.

Lily felt as if she'd been rapped on the bridge of the nose.

"I suppose you do," the man said. He leaned over the counter but stopped short, thank goodness, of touching her.

She was turning into something she abhorred: a woman for whom need was a technique. She wondered how much he would help her. She wiped at her eyes, though they didn't need wiping.

"You don't have to cry," he said.

He told her to wait, and he disappeared down the long rows of filing cabinets, and she stood up straight and did as he'd instructed.

Nikolai was standing in the foyer when she got back to the apartment as if he'd been there since she left, a loyal pet, her own palace guard.

"Where's my surprise?" he asked.

She held up a white bakery box tied with red and white cotton string. He smiled. He loved sweets. He put out his hands, palms up and together. It made him look as if he were offering a shrugging apology. "Grossinger's?" he said. He believed you found the best and stuck with it. He went clear across town to Grossinger's for rum cake, down to the Fillmore East for music, next door to that for Ratner's fresh kosher rolls, up to Jimmy's Soul Food in Harlem for ribs, pickled beet and cucumber salads, and four different types of pudding. Sweet potato was his favorite.

"In the kitchen," Lily said, moving past him.

She put the box on the counter and kept a hand on it, searching a drawer with the other hand for the scissors. He reached across her and tried to rip the string apart. The box creased and bent. "Goddamn Jesus Christ," Nikolai said.

She loved bakery string. She loved its strength and color. She loved the odd little contraption the spools of it hung from next to the register. Who thought of these machines? she often wondered. Who decided what we needed and how to give it to us?

She snipped the string, opened the box, and swiveled it to him as if presenting a diamond necklace in a velvet setting. Inside was a black-and-white cookie. On the white side, a small plastic borzoi stood. Next to it, a shar-pei's tiny paws disappeared into the chocolate icing.

Nikolai peered at them. "You had to meet with the caterer for this?" he asked.

"I didn't meet with the caterer," Lily said.

He was holding the cookie on his flat hand. He looked like a waiter with an impossibly tiny tray. "Do I eat the dogs?" he asked.

Without him, she was doomed. How, after glimpsing this, could she go back to the awkward sons of her mother's friends? The single fathers who sometimes lingered after school, their children dressed for the outdoors, burdened with their backpacks, impatient with fathers and fathers' desires. Any man after this would be merely and devastatingly not Nikolai.

"You didn't graduate from Columbia," she said.

He put the cookie on the counter. The dogs regarded them with their painted eyes. "Who told you that?" he said.

"Tina," she said. "Tina Hernandez," she added.

His eyes were like firecrackers with the sound off.

She put her hand on his. "I know about Tina. I know about Columbia. So don't tell me a story," she said, "unless it's the true one."

He held on to the edge of the counter and leaned in and then away like he was doing push-ups. "That bitch," he said. "That fucking nothing."

He went on like this. There was, she had to admit, something satisfying about hearing him spew such hatred toward that particular woman. It occurred to her that some of it might be performance.

He could've said almost anything. She'd been ready to believe almost anything. But even she was having trouble finding anger and rage reassuring. She was going to have to leave, she thought. Just as she had left Matthew. Someone was trying to make clear that this life was not to be hers.

And then he stopped. He took her by the shoulders and leaned his forehead against hers. "Hold me up," he said.

His need for her was like aloe on her burns. Already his rage was only a moment, something she might've missed if she'd been looking the other way.

His eyes were wet and rimmed with red. "Come," he said, taking her hand, leading her out of the kitchen. "Come to the bedroom, and I will tell you everything."

She was feeling things she knew she shouldn't be feeling under these circumstances. Knowing that made her feel them even more. When she was twelve, she'd taken a long pull off a girl-friend's cigarette and imagined her head as an upside-down moxi-bustion bowl, and had been thrilled, swooning more from her imagination than from the nicotine. She'd reacted afterward with equal melodrama, never smoking again.

Now, she allowed herself to enjoy the small slippery flips her stomach performed at his touch. She followed him through the apartment, turning the lights out on her way.

In the bedroom, he sat on the bed, his hands laced between his knees. He asked her to sit with her back to him as he talked. There were too many things, he said, that made him ashamed.

She did as he asked, perching on the edge of the bed, one foot tucked behind the other calf like a movie star.

"The first lie," he began, as if reading a chapter title. His par-ents had not been murdered by robbers. His mother had been beaten and worked to death by his father. He didn't know why he lied about this. He supposed he was ashamed at not having been able to save her. He'd been only six, but his brother had been only eight, and he'd gone after their father with a small shovel. The blows had not been strong enough to do away with his father right there and then, but he'd died of infections resulting from the injuries. His brother had earned the right to hold his head high. Nikolai had not. This probably had been the reason for their slow and steady drift away from each other during their years at the orphanage. If his brother wanted something, he found a direct way to get it. Nikolai was better at the other ways. They hadn't seen each other since Nikolai had run away from the orphanage.

"What was his name?" Lily asked. Her foot was asleep. She rotated it in small circles.

"Mikhail," he said, as if speaking it too loudly might conjure him.

"It would've been sometimes nice in the life after Russia, to have older brother," he said.

She felt as she did when a favorite preschooler took her aside to whisper something secret: she never knew whether to believe the drama or take it as further evidence of lying. Nikolai continued: The boat trip to America. Staying awake and walking for the whole first day and night in his new country, marveling at his luck, at whatever had allowed him to get this far. The chaos of Times Square, and the way it felt like home.

She began to understand Tina's feelings. It had nothing to do with what he was saying. Here he was, telling her everything, and it was as if a poisonous gas were leaking quietly into the room.

She shook her head. He was talking about reinventing himself, making a background he could be proud of. Did it really matter so much that he had not gone to Columbia? That the money for his first building had come from loan sharks and bookies? Either way, the ending had been the same: He was a success. He was someone who could've gone to Columbia, who could've belonged from the beginning. He loved her.

"Tell me about Tina," she said, turning to face him.

He put his hands over his face, and she thought about the story the Communists told about Chiang Kai-Shek's capture. He had stuck his head in a hole, hoping that if he couldn't see them, they couldn't see him. It was a completely unreliable and unlikely story, but it was retold nonetheless, even by non-Communists like her parents.

"I should've told you about her," he said. He crossed his arms and tucked his hands into his armpits.

She wanted five-senses descriptions, real-life details only an eyewitness could know, and maybe then these pulls at her belly would cease.

"Who else has there been?" she asked.

He looked sad.

"Many, many," he said.

She was grateful for his straightforwardness, but was this where she would have to draw the line and walk away? Was any of what he was saying a deal breaker? She had never before had to ask herself to identify her breaking point.

"I think it's a common thing," he said miserably. "When you lose a mother at an early age."

It might be, she thought. She had no idea.

"Since you, there's been no one," he said. "Only Tina, and she is crazy. When I met you, I told her we were finished, and she said she would kill herself. She said she would kill her children."

Outside, it had been dark for hours. Lily wanted to lie down.

"What should I have done?" he asked as if she might actually answer. "What could I do?"

Only Tina, Lily thought. And Tina is crazy.

"Since you," he said, "there is no one." He took her hand and held it in both of his. "You are everyone," he said.

He'd told her everything and nothing. But she saw Tina gliding smoothly away from them, and that in itself was seductive. Here was Lily's life coming back to her, intact, a penthouse in a new building.

. . .

The note was slipped under the service door when Nikolai was out. Again, no announcement from downstairs. How did this woman move around the building so easily?

It was written on a sheet of lined yellow paper that hadn't been so much folded as stuffed into a plain white envelope. In round, teenage-girl handwriting, it read: "You told him? Now you gotta help me. Please. Please." There was a phone number. "(Between 8 and 4.)"

He'd talked to her. She hadn't realized how much she'd invested in Tina being the one he talked about, not to. The intimacy of the night in their bedroom seeped away, as if guests she hadn't known were in the apartment had filed through the bedroom door one by one, quietly circling the bed. She had an unpleasant image of Nikolai, Tina, and Matthew standing in a little group, talking about her.

Lily reread the note. The "Now" was challenge and accusation. Now that you've told him. It raised issues of responsibility. It made it impossible for her to step away gracefully from somebody else's messy business. You owe me, it said.

She replaced the note in its envelope and slipped it into the pocket of her date book.

When she wasn't teaching, she was planning. It was easy to do nothing about Tina Hernandez and the note she had written. Lists appeared in Lily's notebook, and she rode them like waves.

Once, sitting next to a lovely gay man in his flower store, choosing centerpieces, she'd had to fight the urge to tell him about Tina and Nikolai and this feeling that sometimes bubbled to her throat.

Another time, she'd passed Saint Patrick's and had made it all the way to the confessional before remembering that she wasn't Catholic.

One afternoon, around the sand table with Gabriel, her favorite boy, his hair a mess of wiry dreadlocks, she asked him how you could tell if someone was lying. He passed her a plastic dinosaur and told her to bury it.

Her parents made her crazy with feelings of impatience and arrogance and a vague childhood sense that she'd done something wrong. She began to see the wedding as the beginning of her life without them and all that they made her feel.

She began formulating sentences in her mind, all of which began with: *When I get married.*

She started avoiding her own apartment, spending more and more time at his. She began making a habit of waking him in the middle of the night for lovemaking. At first, he was thrilled, and then he began to tease her, holding his hands in prayer. "Have mercy," he said.

On a Friday morning in early February, ten days before the wedding, she stepped around the corner of Madison on her way to the crosstown bus, and there was Tina. She had two girls with her. They looked about three and four, almost twins. Two large backpacks dwarfed them. They had matching hats and scarves, rainbow-colored with pom-poms at the ends of them and the tips of the hats. They stood on either side of their mother, holding her bare hands with mittened ones. They could've been Lily's students.

Tina's hair was not the art object it had been the last time. It was pulled back into a ponytail. She wore dusty pink sweatpants and a man's black sweater beneath her open coat. Her face was clean. She looked like she had many things to do in a very short amount of time.

"How are you?" Lily asked, glancing at the clock on the bank behind them. She stressed the *are,* as if she'd just been in the midst of thinking about Tina's well-being.

"He won't leave me alone," she said.

Lily's heart thumped. For a moment, she misunderstood.

Tina took her hands away from the girls' and held out the edges of her coat like the Ghost of Christmas Present. "Hang on to this," she said.

Lily watched the girls grab hold. She's a mother, she thought.

Tina reached into the neck of her sweater and pulled out a key on a shoelace. In that one gesture, Tina became twelve, coming home from school by herself, letting herself into an empty apartment. Lily's friends with working mothers had had shoelaces just like it. She'd envied them for their access to grown-up worlds without the grown-ups.

Tina balled up the key and lace and held it out to Lily. "Three fifty-five Riverside Drive," she said. "A Hundred and Eighth street. Apartment three C."

Lily couldn't bring herself to reach for it.

"Mama," the older girl said, tugging on the coat. "We're gonna be late."

Tina palmed the girl's head. The girl relaxed, as if her mother had given her an answer.

"It's a place he keeps," she said.

Lily overheated in the winter air. She could feel sweat between her breasts. "I don't want that," she said.

Tina kept her fist out. "I understand you don't wanna help me," she said. "But if I'm in trouble, you're in trouble." She took Lily's hand and held it as if she were going to read her palm. "Help yourself," she said. "Seems like you're good at that."

Lily took it. She put it around her own neck, tucking it into her turtleneck. It was warm against her chest. She thought of Nikolai's way of humming against her skin as he kissed her.

"There's a journal," Tina said. "In the bottom drawer of the oven. He took it from someone's apartment. You read it," she said.

She didn't seem crazy. She didn't seem needy. She was scared, and even through her fear, concerned for Lily. It made Lily know that both the concern and the fear were genuine.

"Come on, girls," Tina said. "Say good-bye to Ms. Chin."

"Good-bye, Ms. Chin," the girls sang out in unison, and then they were gone.

Lily stood. Passersby made moving around her a noisy event. They wanted her to know she was inconveniencing them. An old woman walking a small dog in a red sweater and matching booties told her to step to one side or the other.

 at school, she found a note and a phone message from Matthew. She wasn't surprised. The note said: "Answer your phone." The message said: "Come find me." Was everyone going to be leaving her notes? She did not have time for Matthew.

She made it through lunch. As she and the assistant teacher sat in their tiny chairs pulled up to the tiny tables, helping the children pour their own juice out of plastic measuring cups into paper cups, she held her stomach and told her assistant that she didn't feel well, she thought she had better go home.

There was much concern from the other teacher and the children. "Do you have a headache?" Gabriel asked. "My mother has headaches."

She was asked if she wanted to throw up, to poop. Concern was voiced about who would take care of the class.

The assistant teacher began a long and captivating narrative about how the rest of the day would go, and Lily slipped out into the gray afternoon.

Three fifty-five Riverside Drive was on the corner, an almost-grand building of yellow brick with subtle architectural flourishes. Not the kind Nikolai liked. Not even the kind he'd own, and he had very few criteria for those.

She stood outside it until children coming home from school gave her looks.

There was no doorman, just two sets of double glass doors, one propped open with a piece of wood. The lock on the inside doors was duct-taped. Lily scanned a panel of nameplates and buzzers for the apartment numbers. The name next to 3C read Carpanetti.

The elevator was old, a brass door with a porthole window.

Every now and then one of the numbers lit up the way it was supposed to.

A man and a teenage girl came into the lobby just as Lily stepped into the elevator. She recognized him from work. He was a teacher in the upper school. "Sam," the man said to the girl, "hold the elevator." Lily held the door for them. The girl, beautiful and blond, thanked her and told her father to hurry up. They pressed eight, and the father watched Lily press three. He had a Channel Thirteen tote bag over his shoulder. He was the kind of guy who carried tote bags and believed in raising his blond daughter in this neighborhood.

He smiled at her, a stranger being nice.

"I'm visiting someone," she said.

He raised his eyebrows. "That's nice," he said. He smoothed his daughter's hair absentmindedly.

There was something sad about both of them. Lily found herself wondering where the mother was.

The door opened on three, and Lily strode out, turning left and walking down the long hallway until the elevator was gone and she could stop and get her bearings.

The smells were the smells of all Upper West Side buildings. Curries and stews. Grease. Cleaning fluids.

3C was at the end of the hallway. She listened at the door. She knocked and waited. The key fit and turned easily.

The front hall was small and bare. She shivered.

The kitchen was to her left, closet-sized, with a skinny window looking out to the next building. The appliances were sized for tiny people. The oven drawer moved easily, as if recently oiled. There between a roasting pan and a cookie sheet was the journal.

Why did he have a cookie sheet here? she wondered. Did he make cookies?

Should she take the journal or read it here? She marveled at how little she had thought this all out. She panned her mind for his schedule today. Her mind was a windless plain. She never knew his schedule. She didn't really even know what he did all day. What did someone who owned buildings do? Did he spend his time perusing a table spread with glossy photos of tall buildings?

The journal was soft-covered, fake leather. 1976 was embossed on the front in gold. A red flat cord hung from its seam. She smoothed her hand over the cover.

She should go. Who knew who might show up here? People she didn't want to meet. People she didn't want to know about.

The central room was filling with afternoon light. There were two armchairs and a Danish-looking couch. Some attempts had been made at furniture arrangement. The two walls without windows were lined with pressboard bookcases. The shelves sagged with books. She'd had no idea he was such a reader but understood that it made perfect sense. The books bothered her more than the bed. On her way here she'd imagined the unmade bed with its unfamiliar sheets. *This is where he goes*, she'd thought, *with his many, many others*.

But now, she wanted to weep. This was not a place he went to be with others. This was a place he went to be with himself. Occasionally, it was clear, he let others in. But it was a haven from his daily life. Lily was part of his other world. She was whatever the opposite of haven was.

The elevator door opened. Footsteps were coming down the hall.

She sat on the couch facing the door and straightened her back, the journal on her thighs. This is how he'll find me, she thought.

A door opened and closed, the locks tumbling back into place.

She opened the journal. It was not his handwriting. It was not his name in the upper right-hand corner of the first page. Of course it wasn't. Tina had said he'd taken it from someone's apartment. *Gina Engel,* in the kind of writing that suggested penmanship classes, exercise books with dotted lines.

Lily felt something let go. She hadn't wanted to read Nikolai's journal. Gina Engel's journal? That was fine. How bad could that be? Immediately, the feeling that had let go grabbed hold again. Tina had wanted her to read this for a reason. Things could always be worse than you'd imagined.

The day and date were printed on the top of every page. Under that was a count of the number of days in the year left to go. *32nd Day—333 days to follow.* It was the kind of thing you might do in prison. In the other corner of each page, a small box with four choices: Clear, Cloudy, Rain, Snow. A box was always checked, even when whole weeks were skipped, their pages blank.

Lily read. The sun dipped lower behind her, getting darker and cooler as it fell. Dust motes floated around her.

Gina Engel had a son named Steven and an ex-husband who lived in San Diego. She tried to be polite about him, even in her journal, but Lily could tell they didn't get along.

Steven had hair like a boy Gina had known in grade school, still had some of his baby teeth, and smelled like the air off the river, the plastic of the models he liked to build, and the beginning of teenage boy. Gina worried about him. He was somber, moody, secretive. Pages went by without a mention of him. It wasn't clear what any of this had to do with her or Nikolai or Tina.

There was someone named Phil who came up a lot, and other men. Details about meeting them. About going home with them, during the day mostly, when Steven was at school. Sometimes at night, when Steven was at a friend's. Sometimes they came over after he went to sleep. Their names came up, then disappeared, then came up again. Or didn't.

Sometimes Gina Engel dramatized whole scenes as if fulfilling an assignment. Lily was put off by her style. Flowery adjectives, too many adverbs.

There were arguments with Phil. A long story about someone named Kurt who'd stayed until four in the morning and who wanted to make love to her on the living room floor, but Steven had been asleep in the bedroom, so they'd gone downstairs to Kurt's car on Riverside Drive.

She registered that Gina Engel lived near her.

Kurt and Gina made love against the open passenger door, laughing and whispering, and then Gina had rushed back up to her apartment, using her son as her excuse. The next day Kurt called to tell her the car door was broken. By the following week, she didn't want to see him anymore. She didn't return his calls; she told Steven to tell him she wasn't there. He came to her window one evening, standing in the middle of the street, calling her name. She pulled Steven down to the floor, telling him it was just some guy who thought he was in love with her. They crawled beneath the windows, and she let Steven peek up over the sill. "He's talking to Manuel," Steven reported. "He looks sad," Steven said.

"Why does he think he's in love with you?" he asked. Gina hadn't recorded her answer.

She worked as a nurse in a hospital. She didn't say which. She felt lucky to have the job, but she didn't get up every morning thrilled with where she was heading. Lily got the sense that for a long time her son had been enough, and now maybe he wasn't.

She didn't understand why Tina had wanted her to read this.

She flipped ahead. There were pages in May missing. They'd been precisely extracted so close to the spine that she didn't even notice at first. The same thing for the first week in August. Gina Engel's last entry was on August 10.

Steven to Juan's. It's like we're guests at the same hotel. One day I'll wake up and he'll have checked out.

Thinking of calling in sick.

9—Ice cream with Phil.

It was four twenty. She got Tina's card out of her date book, picked up the phone, and called.

A man with an accent answered. She asked if she could please speak with Tina Hernandez. Nervousness made her excessively polite.

The man wanted to know who was calling.

The feeling that she was lying filled her throat. "Lily Chin," she said.

"Lily Chin?" he repeated. And then he said it again. "From three F?"

She shouldn't have given her real name. "Yes," she said. "May I ask with whom I am speaking?"

"It's Manuel," he said. "From the building. The eight-to-four guy," he said.

She was watching a schoolyard full of children race ahead of her to the good swings.

"I'm sorry," she said. "I must have the wrong number, though it's lovely to talk to you."

He laughed. "No, no. You got the right number; Tina's not here. I didn't know you and my wife were—well, knew each other." He was curious, not suspicious, willing to have everything explained.

Lily didn't know what to say. Nikolai was sleeping with his doorman's wife. She knew she should be concentrating on other things, but she just kept coming back to his doorman's wife.

"I met her on the street the other day," she said. "She was with your girls. They were sweet." She wasn't lying. They were. She had.

"Yeah," he said. "Taking years off my life," he said warmly.

Your wife is sleeping with my fiancé, she thought. She realized abruptly that she'd continued to think of Nikolai and Tina in the present tense.

She cleared her throat. "I actually just have a quick question. I lost the address and number of a friend of mine that Tina knows."

"Tina knows a friend of yours?" he asked.

Her lies tumbled around her like bricks off a tall building. He's a doorman, she thought. He's not an idiot.

She couldn't imagine anything but to keep going. "Gina Engel?" she said. "Do you know her?"

There was silence, and for a moment Lily thought he'd put down the phone and walked away.

"Did you?" he asked. His voice had gotten clipped.

She wanted to know about Gina Engel more than she wanted to get off the phone. "I haven't seen her in a long time. I'm trying to reconnect."

He exhaled. It came out like a whistle. "She died," he said. "Murdered the summer before last. I'm sorry."

Breathe, she told herself. Think. She closed her eyes. Of course, she thought. Of course. Gina Engel. She remembered now. The woman from her block. She sat there, silent and stupid.

"How did you know her?" he asked.

She commanded her mind to work. Possibilities and implications took slow shape. It was like watching a water ballet. The best lies were the ones closest to the truth. She remembered a school friend telling her that once.

"I knew her son," she said. "Steven," she added. He went to her school. She knew all kinds of children.

"Steven was a good boy," he said as if arguing with her.

He gave her the details of the case that she remembered from the newspapers. But something about him kept her wary. She was the girl in the house alone in a horror movie. It was just a feeling.

"Did they catch the guy?" she asked.

"Not yet," he said. "They never even found the weapon."

"Do they know anything about him?" she asked.

"Not really," he said. "Someone she knew, they think. Maybe someone she was, you know, *with*."

Nikolai. She remembered the photo the papers had run. Dark hair. Dark eyes. Good Mediterranean skin hidden under too much makeup. Someone who didn't think she was as attractive as she was. She imagined Nikolai with her. So what? she thought vehemently. So he slept with someone who was murdered. That was all.

She swept her mind for what a normal person should say in this situation. "That's horrible," she said. "The whole thing is horrible."

"Yeah," he said, as if she couldn't have articulated the problem more eloquently. "Tina's been in a real mess over it all."

"Yes," Lily said. "Of course. Yes." She slid her finger along the edges of the missing journal pages. She was suddenly hungry. Could she ask how he knew Gina Engel, or was that something she should already know? How did people spend their lives as liars? How did they keep track of it all?

She felt like she'd made a prank call that had backfired. "I'll try Tina later then," she said.

"Okay," he said. "I'm sorry," he said again.

"That's okay," she said. "It's not your fault," she said, and she meant it. She replaced the receiver in its cradle and hung her head between her legs.

matthew was where she knew he would be. On top of the double stairs above the side entrance to the Museum of Natural History. They had gone here often late at night during the months they had been together. It was a staircase that led to nowhere, and felt temporary in a permanent way, like a construction site after hours.

He was bouncing lightly on the balls of his feet, holding a cigarette with all four fingers and thumb in that way of his. When he saw her, he flicked it away. There were several others already on the ground.

His cheek, when she palmed it, was cold and dry. He closed his eyes, leaned into her hand, and covered it with his. He had always been able to make her feel as if his need for her had twin proportions to hers. In someone so entitled, so lucky in terms of what life had to offer, it always surprised her. Reminded her how difficult it was to know someone with anything like real confidence, how much of a blessing it was to receive even a glimpse behind the curtains of someone you loved.

Her hand was still on his cheek. What was she doing here? What did she want from him?

With his eyes still closed, he said, "Days aren't days without you. Life without you is stupid and impossible."

She wrapped her arms around him beneath his coat. She worked her hands under his shirt and placed her fingertips in the small of his back, where they had discovered, years ago, a spot built just for them.

She was not herself. She was some version of herself that knowing these two men had brought to the surface. Maybe that meant she was *more* herself.

"Let's pretend," she said. "Let's pretend we're making love for the first time."

He was kissing the corners of her mouth. The tip of his tongue moved under her lip.

"It's always the first time," he said.

"No," she said, feeling his shoulder blades, the scar from the tractor accident, the mole on his stomach. "The first time. Do you remember?" She didn't want approximation, she wanted recreation.

His knee and thigh moved between her legs, as they had years ago against her apartment door. She closed her eyes and let him undress her only as much as they had then. She opened his belt, the same one, she was sure, he'd been wearing then. He moved inside of her, and again, his mouth found her ear, and she shivered, anticipating. He asked quietly, "Whadja get for me?" The childlike desire made her feel as if she were being pulled from quicksand.

And she was grateful, as she had been then, but this time she knew what she wanted. She wanted to be in control, to have a say in how at least one thing in her life would resolve itself. So when they were done, she would tell him he must leave her alone, and his face would register more surprise than sadness. He would leave her alone, and he would be fine without her. And perhaps she would teach him what he had taught her: that the least likely people are capable of the most unexpected things.

eight

The next night, Lily and Nikolai took the Town Car out to Queens for her parents' annual Chinese New Year party. The Year of the Horse. A time of change, a crossroads. The end of the bad; the beginning of the good. Lily believed very little of it.

They spoke of the usual things. Nikolai held her hand, playing with her fingers as he always did whenever in moving vehicles.

She watched his fingers until she couldn't watch them anymore. She leaned back against the seat and concentrated on the sky rushing by.

He blinked his eyelashes against her cheek. "Butterfly kisses," he said. He spread his fingertips across her kneecap. "Starfish." He rubbed the tip of her nose with his thumb. "Eskimo," he said.

"Not with your thumb," she said without looking at him. "With your nose."

She closed her eyes. *Nikolai*, she thought. *Nikolai and his little-boy games*. Gina Engel's newspaper photo spread across her mind like water.

He rubbed her nose again with his thumb. "Iguanadon," he said.

"I never know what you're talking about," she said sleepily.

"Dinosaurs," he said into her hair. "Big thumbs."

"How do you know this stuff?" she asked. Her eyes were still closed. An image of those bookshelves filled her mind. Her stomach felt as if they'd taken a turn too quickly. In her mind, she formulated one question in various ways.

He didn't answer. He sang softly into her hair. Something Italian. How did he know Italian?

"What did you do yesterday?" he asked.

The cold air on the museum's terrace moved through her. She repeated the question in her mind, straining to read his tone.

"Work," she said.

He was still humming.

"What else would I be doing?" she asked. How had her life become a spy movie?

"Of course," he said. "Friday."

When she was six, her parents had taken her to the July Fourth fireworks. They'd explained what she'd see, her father lecturing her about the art of fire—a Chinese invention when a cook had mixed sulfur, charcoal, and saltpeter. But they hadn't told her about the noise. She'd been startled by sound she could feel. She'd fallen asleep against her father. They'd covered her ears, and she'd slept through the entire show.

Now, she rested her head against Nikolai's mouth, watched the wires of the bridge flashing by, and hoped for sleep.

"You should quit your job," Nikolai said softly.

Lily kept staring out the window. There was the bridge. There was the water.

"You're getting married," he said. "You don't need to work."

She sat up. She regarded the back of the driver's head. He was wearing a blue cap. Nikolai liked the drivers to wear caps.

"I *like* to work," she said.

He brushed something invisible from his pants. "You do," he said, as if congratulating her on her insight. "But that's not so much the point," he said.

"It's not?" she asked.

He smiled.

"Why are you smiling?" she asked.

The driver glanced in the rearview mirror.

"You're mad," he said, still smiling.

"What about the children?" she asked. "You don't just leave a classroom full of three-year-olds without any warning." She was filled with righteousness, with a mother's mock surprise. Don't you know better than this? Use your brain. Be a smart boy.

Beneath the righteousness was what she imagined to be beneath a mother's surface as well: fear. Fear at doing or saying the thing that would end up making all the difference. She saw herself as witness to an apocalypse of her child's doing. I didn't know. He always seemed so quiet. It's not my fault.

He put his hand beneath her skirt and smoothed his way up her stockinged thigh. "You are mad, and I am hard," he said as if memorizing their names.

She held his wrist. "Don't," she said. "It's not good."

They turned onto her parents' block. Their door and stoop were decorated with red lanterns and banners with the characters for longevity and good luck in gold. Chinese people milled around on the sidewalk. She could hear the gongs.

He put his face close to hers and squeezed her inner thigh.

It was not what he was doing or saying. It was a feeling. She was in the open doorway of an airplane.

He was the ground rushing toward her.

Then he sat back and shrugged. "Okeydokey. You want to work? You work," he said as if none of this had been his idea in the first place.

She breathed again. He was her parachute.

He was the only white person at the party. Her parents were thrilled with him. Her mother ushered him here and there, introducing him to all her lady friends. They squeezed his forearms. He laughed, he smiled, he kissed them on both cheeks. Sometimes he hugged them, lifted them off their tiny feet.

He got drunk on Maotai with her father, and the two of them sang a loud, center-stage performance of "Sunrise, Sunset." Her father knew none of the words but murmured along gamely, smiling shyly next to this man who must have seemed more like a bear than a son.

Nikolai was like a tree on a plain of shrubs. She basked in the association. The daughters of her mother's friends regarded her from across the room, occasionally tilting their black shiny heads toward each other to whisper like the chorus in an opera. The sons lined up to congratulate her, glad for the chance for any kiss with any girl under any circumstances.

It was a certain kind of going-away party. Like they were watching her step onto a rocket ship for a trip they were willing to believe could be worthwhile, though they hadn't yet figured out how.

At one in the morning they finally left. She'd never known her parents to stay up this late. They were red-faced from the wine as they walked them to the car. Her mother hugged her, told her she loved her, and reminded her how lucky she was.

"Be glad," she said. "Feel lucky."

"Ma," Lily protested, pulling back to look at her. So much of her mother's life had not been her own. "What am I going to do?"

Her mother hushed her. "You always thinking something."

The driver held the door open. Lily felt as if her mother had been at the museum the night before.

"Don't think," her mother said, ushering Lily into the car.

Go to the West Side," Nikolai told the driver.

The driver seemed to know what he meant.

Nikolai pulled her to him. "I want to take you somewhere," he said.

He opened the door with his own key. Hers was in her bag, wrapped in its shoelace.

The apartment was as she had left it the day before. He gave her a tour. She watched him for signs that he was seeing through her performance.

She found herself in tears.

He put down the photo of his eighteen-year-old self he was showing her. "Why are you crying?" he asked. "It's not good?"

She pressed her eyelids with her fingertips. She thought of what she could say. She thought of Matthew. That was a colossal betrayal, and it might be the least of the problems between them.

She thought of the journal in the oven drawer beneath the cookie sheet. She thought of Gina Engel. She feared she would never stop thinking of Gina Engel.

Finally, she said simply, "I'm glad you showed me this place."

She could see relief in his eyes. He had been worried, she thought. He had been worried about her reaction. Maybe Gina Engel had been one of the many. That meant only that, nothing more.

"What we want, we'll move to our apartment," he said. "I don't need this place anymore."

Would this be what Tina had done to them? A lifetime of Nikolai offering her exactly what she wanted; a lifetime of her inability to trust his offerings?

No, she thought. Things could always be worse. To find the truth, she had become someone who lied. Here he was making his offerings, and her own lies spread out on their surface like an oil spill.

Tell him, she thought. Tell him about fear and worry, how they feel and what they can make you do.

He pulled her onto the rug and took her shoes off and palmed her feet, pressing her arch in the spot that was always sore.

The rug smelled of books and cigars, and the other smells of this small country of his. Just yesterday they had been completely new. Today they were already known.

She opened her mouth to ask him her questions, to raise her confusions and have them eliminated. Just tell me, she would say to one of her hesitant preschoolers. If you don't tell me, I can't help you. She imagined all the times a child had released his secrets and she still hadn't been able to help. Did she really want his secrets? Did she really want to share hers?

"What are you doing?" he asked, looking up at her, lifting her hips, rolling her panty hose off with the palms of his hands. He opened and closed his mouth, imitating her.

"Carp kisses," she said.

She believed she could never know if the person she was promising to spend the rest of her life with was the right person with whom to make that promise. All she could do was stack whatever odds she could in her favor, not do anything stupid, and hope for the best.

She would neither ask her questions nor seek his answers nor offer her own, and that knowledge made her sadder than she'd been since Tina had rung the doorbell. She was breaking all her rules. She was not stacking odds in her favor, and she was doing something stupid. And all of that made it impossible to hope for the best. She hadn't earned the right to hope for the best.

Monday it snowed. School was postponed and then canceled. Nikolai said he would stay home with her. She told him she had far too much to do to have him underfoot. She stood with him in the foyer, tying his scarf the way he liked it. She thought that the more days she put between Friday and now, the more chance she had of living this life.

"You're trying to get rid of me," he said. He was smiling.

"You're right," she said. She stood on her toes to kiss him. She palmed the side of his face. Its smoothness was always surprising. He seemed like the kind of man who should have rough skin.

He kissed her back and pressed them against the wall. His

framed prints rearranged themselves with small noises. When he hugged her like this, his need for her was something she could hold.

"The other day," he said. "Friday. Did you go by your apartment during the day?"

She opened her eyes over his shoulder. In the mirror, she could see the back of his head, her fingers lost in his hair.

"I don't remember," she said. "Why?"

He shrugged. "Someone thought they saw you wandering around the West Side."

"Someone?" she said. The papers had said Gina Engel had been stabbed. Her son had found her in the foyer.

He was still holding her.

He rubbed his hand back and forth across the small of her back. "A guy who works with me," he said.

He bundled her hair in his hand and tugged gently. "So, were you wandering?"

"I *work* on the West Side," she said. She tried to pull back. He wasn't moving. The corner of a frame was pressing into her shoulder blade. "Are you following me?" Her tone was not what she'd intended. She glanced at the front door. It was double-locked.

"You betcha," he said, pulling her head back, leaning down to take her chin in his mouth. "I'm following you. I'm having you followed."

He reached his hand down the back of her jeans and slid his finger inside of her.

"I know your every move," he said, closing his mouth over hers.

She closed her eyes and a groan moved up her throat. Fear, arousal, she hadn't been able to tell the difference in weeks.

.   .   .

as soon as she was alone, she bundled up and left, having given him enough time to get out of the area. Manuel was not on the door. She hadn't seen him since their phone conversation.

Already the snow was to the tops of her boots. She bent her head against the large wet flakes.

At a phone booth she huddled over the phone as if over a campfire. She held up a gloved finger, ready to disconnect if Manuel answered.

It rang and rang. The answering machine clicked on. Manuel's voice. "Please. If this is Tina. Please. Tell me where you are. I'll come for you. Wherever you are, I'll come."

Lily hung up.

The snow eddied around the booth. Her whole world was this one ratty phone booth.

The street was undisturbed snow. A woman in a red ski suit glided by on cross-country skis.

Had Tina walked out on Manuel? Had he found out about Nikolai?

Her mind expanded and contracted. The other possibilities moved through her like a pulse.

She opened the booth door and threw up into the snow.

She walked to the 19th Precinct on Sixty-seventh Street and stood across from it. One officer was shoveling. Another was watching, rocking back and forth, heel to toe, hands in pockets, like a parody of a cop on a stoop.

She tried to decide if he seemed friendly. Parked cars had been transformed into rolling hills. Children were sledding down town house stoops.

The cops started lobbing snowballs at each other. Unbelievably, she found herself laughing.

They noticed her. A snowball floated across the street in a high arc and landed at her feet.

She made another one and threw it back. She had never thrown a snowball before. And because she couldn't imagine what she would say to these two men, couldn't imagine where to begin, she didn't say anything. Instead, she stood across the street for a few minutes, pitching, winging—all those verbs that she'd never been the subject for—not-so-well-packed snowballs at two handsome young cops, no one saying a word, all of them smiling like children.

She walked across the park and uptown to her place. She hadn't been there in days, and she knew when she opened the door that someone had been there in her absence. The smells were wrong. The hallway light was on.

She tried to decipher the disturbances. It went without saying that nothing like this had ever happened to her before, or maybe even found lodging in her imagination. So there was something almost wonderful about it, as if she had been walking along and someone had taken her face and turned her toward something that was available and possible, all the things she'd been missing by looking only straight ahead. It wasn't a completely healthy reaction, but it was the one she experienced nonetheless, and she felt it was only fair and honest to recognize it as such.

The two chairs on either side of the small dining table were angled away from the table and each other as if they'd argued. There was a fresh half-gallon of skim milk in the fridge. A brand she never bought. The bok choy she'd left in the vegetable crisper was there, limp and wet, a new pint of robust cherry tomatoes next to it.

The bed had been remade. The sheets and blankets hung, untucked, off the sides and ends. The pillows were at the foot.

Her drawers, the old trunk in the closet, the shoeboxes on the closet shelf had all been gone through. The lids sat skewed like awkward smiles.

Matthew was not a possibility. It was Nikolai. She could smell his aftershave. It came in a dark glass bottle shaped like a polished rock, and she liked it so much that she used it herself on occasion.

It didn't surprise her. He was sending her a message about intimacy. It was the same part of him that insisted on dropping by friends' apartments unannounced, walking into coworkers' offices without knocking.

There were crumbs around the toilet. He liked to snack while using the bathroom. Her hand towel was not hanging on its hook. She knew she would find it wherever he had gone next.

She did not know how threatening she should find the message he was sending.

She brushed her teeth, avoiding herself in the mirror.

She imagined telling someone that the first thing she'd done upon discovering that her apartment had been searched in her absence by her fiancé was to brush her teeth. She imagined telling someone that he'd searched her apartment. She did not want to think about Gina Engel.

Maybe this would be her life, she thought. Her husband would present her with his varied and slightly menacing oddities.

Oddities, she understood grimly, might be the wrong word to describe what was going on here. Or it might, she understood equally grimly, be the perfect word.

She spit, rinsed, sat on the toilet. Her mind was not made for this kind of problem. She could barely get her mind around the physics of weather. Reading the installation instructions for her stereo system had made her anxious and sleepy.

But one way or the other, she was going to have to do something. There was no getting around that.

She tried to think of people she admired. What would they do?

She tried to think of someone who would not look at her in disbelief, who would not say, touching a concerned hand to her forearm, Of course, you know you have to leave him. You know that you've stayed this long is not a good sign.

"I find Nikolai Belov completely admirable," she said to the ceiling. She closed her eyes and repeated the sentence quietly to herself, switching back and forth between past and present tense.

She went to the window. Outside, it was early afternoon and still snowing. At those children's concerts her parents had taken her to at Lincoln Center, behind the musicians a giant pad of paper ran the length of the stage. A woman ran here and there in sensible shoes, drawing to the music with a thick black marker. Her shoes made soft thumps on the wooden stage. Lily had liked listening for them.

She put her palm to the glass. The snow took no notice.

Was she trapped or protected?

She went to the phone and dialed Nikolai. His phone rang. One way or another, there would be answers. She reminded herself that she was the kind of woman who could take solace in what she had.

Take solace, she told herself. It's what you do best.

nine

On her way to meet him, she walked by Gina Engel's building. It was on the same block as hers, closer to the park.

The snow blew off the river. She walked with her eyes closed. There was no one else on the sidewalk, and she was moving too slowly to hurt herself. She stopped by a man trying to dig his car out. He stabbed his shovel into some snow, sat next to it, and stared into space.

This whole part of the sidewalk had been taped off after the murder. She hadn't known what had happened until the next morning when she'd gone to do her shopping. She'd met Muriel Yablonsky from 8D on her way back. "You met her," Muriel had reminded her. "At the block party." Lily didn't remember. "Yes," Muriel insisted. "Her son got lost." Then Lily did. She hadn't liked her.

After Muriel gave her the details, Lily remembered thinking that she hadn't asked to know any of it.

She'd been stopped on the street twice—once by a detective and once by a reporter. Both men's lack of enthusiasm matched her own. No, she hadn't seen anything unusual. No, she didn't know the woman or her son. Yes, she lived alone, and no, she told the reporter, she wasn't more worried now about that.

She'd had one dream about the murder, and when she woke with a start in the middle of the night, she'd strained to remember it, knowing that was the surest way to watch it slip away for good.

A window in Gina Engel's building opened and a woman's head and torso appeared. She was an older woman, but her hair had been dyed jet black and was styled around her head in soft waves. She called down to the street. "Almost?" she said.

"Almost," he called back, not moving from his hill.

The woman disappeared; the window slid shut.

She wondered if Nikolai had come here often. She wondered how they'd met. Had he been introduced to Steven? What had Steven thought of him?

She imagined a sleepy boy stumbling down the hall to the bathroom in the middle of the night, running into Nikolai, naked and carrying two whiskey glasses down the hall.

What was wrong with her? Other people's narratives were just that—other people's.

What would she ask him? She didn't want to have the conversation they had to have. She wanted to be on the other side of it.

Snow made epaulets on her shoulders. It fell off her hat.

The man with the shovel regarded her. "So," he said, looking up at the thick sky. "Snow."

She nodded. She'd seen him around the block.

"You just standing?" he said.

"I'm waiting for someone," she said.

He nodded.

She wished she hadn't said anything. Now what would she do?

Nikolai wasn't meeting her here. She'd have to walk away, pretend she'd been stood up. Minutes would have to pass before she could do that.

He regarded her. "Don't I know you?"

Matthew's face and voice appeared for her. "I don't think so," she said.

He was unpersuaded. "I know you."

She shrugged.

"I live here with Mommy," he said, gesturing toward the window that had opened.

He was a grown man. It seemed charming and creepy at the same time. He was wearing blue sweatpants and a gray sweatshirt. His hair came out from under the hood. It was below his shoulders, straight and brown. He was wearing athletic socks with plastic sandals. In the snow.

"You like baseball?" he asked.

Lily checked her watch. She needed to move on. Nikolai would be waiting.

"I like the Yankees," the man said. "They're the crème de la crème of the baseball world." He held his hand up like he was measuring someone tall.

She could barely follow this conversation. She registered her surprise at his vocabulary. Snob, she thought. You are a horrible person.

"Sixth game of the series, nineteen seventy-seven," he said. "Bleacher seats, a post right in front of them. I was supposed to go with this girl from the building. Said she was a fan, but something came up, so I scalped her ticket. Guess how much I made?"

Nothing was really required of her in terms of a response.

He stood up. His pants were soaked. His feet must've been numb.

"One-five-oh," he said. He made an "okay" sign. "Man," he said. He seemed happy thinking about it.

He hadn't made eye contact during the entire conversation.

She took a step back. "I've got to go," she said. "I just remembered."

He held his hands up like he was surrendering. "Sure," he said. "You go." He picked up his shovel. "Maybe I could give you a call," he said. "You know, sometime."

Lily brushed the snow off her coat, shook out her hat. "Oh," she said. "I'm going to have a husband."

"Sure, sure," he called as she walked away. "Bring your husband," he said. "Come by anytime. I'm here mostly."

She kept herself from running. He was just lonely. Lonely *was* threatening, she thought. For the first time, she felt shame at what she had done to Matthew. She assuaged the guilt by reminding herself that he liked to believe he needed people more than he actually did.

She bowed her head and watched her feet make their thick march through the snow. She was not like that. She did not want to be a person who was lonely. She did not want to be a person who was alone. "I'm going to have a husband," she said to her feet. "I'm going to have a husband."

Nikolai had wanted to meet at his West Side place. She was late, but he wasn't there yet.

She used Tina's key. What's one more thing to explain? she

thought. She would tell all, he would too, and they would go on together and alone, leaving Matthew Cullen and Tina Hernandez and Gina Engel and all the rest at the gate.

He'd already started packing up. She tried to guess which piles were to be saved. She hoped that he'd chosen what she would've chosen. The photo of young Nikolai, the samovar.

She checked the oven drawer. The journal was gone. It was becoming impossible to keep track of the possibilities of the situation. She needed a flow chart.

She wandered back into the living room with the cookie sheet and put it on what she felt sure was a throwaway pile.

A collection of postcards was stacked in piles, a cityscape beneath the glass coffee table. Next to the postcards was a box of note cards. Black-and-white photographs of Asian foods. A bowl of noodles, a pork bun, a custard tart, dumplings. One of the envelopes had "Steven" written in block letters on it. It was a picture of a bowl of rice. Inside, in the same block letters: "I think of you often and wish you well."

The door swung open, hitting the wall hard. Nikolai was there, a gun in his hand.

"Lily," he said, somewhere between anger and relief. "How did you get in here?"

"You have a gun?" she asked. She was sitting on the floor. The gun was small and black.

He slid it into his coat pocket, unbuttoned the coat, and flapped the snow from the black cashmere like a bird contemplating flight. "Everyone has a gun," he said.

Even the boys she'd known in high school, the Chinese ones in Chinese gangs, hadn't had guns.

He was standing over her. He smelled of snow and vaguely of gasoline.

"I don't think that's true," she said, standing.

He shrugged.

"How did you get in?" he asked. His dress shoes were soaked and looked permanently misshapen. He'd left the house in them this morning even though it had already been snowing for hours. His closet was lined with multiple pairs of the same shoes in black and brown. She'd never seen him in anything else.

She reached into her pocket and pulled out the key. "Tina's," she said.

"Okay then," he said. He shook out of his coat and threw it over a chair. He toed his shoes off and pulled his socks off inside-out.

He held his hand out. She held his eye and handed over the key.

"I'll make tea," he said, heading to the kitchen.

It had only been this morning when she'd seen him last, but she felt as if she'd been alone for days. Here he was, someone with opinions and counterarguments of his own. He had a gun. It made her thoughts tumble out of formation like unruly children. She thought about padding by the kitchen door, letting herself out. She thought about staying put and lying about what she wanted to talk about. She could tell him she wanted to elope. By tomorrow, they could be married.

He came back in carrying a mug for her, a cup and saucer for himself. She watched him sip from the black cup, his fingers too large for the delicate handle. He looked like a trained animal.

Her heartbeat was thumping in her head. What did she want most? Most people passed their whole lives without even asking this question. He sat on the couch and patted the seat next to him. He seemed to feel there wasn't a surprising thing she could say, but that was okay because surprises had not been her draw in the first place.

A strategy she used with the preschoolers came to her. Don't demand. Ask. Let them think it's you who need the help, they who hold the solutions.

Just tell the truth, her father used to say to her.

"I'm confused," she said. This was the truth. "And I need your help figuring things out."

He sat up like this was some kind of quiz.

"I need for you to tell me about you and Gina Engel. I need to know why Tina Hernandez would want me to read Gina Engel's journal. I need to know why you even had it. I need to know what you were looking for in my apartment. I need to know why you're having me followed."

And once the litany was under way, the big question stepped forward as if standing in the wings the entire time. "I need to know that you had nothing to do with Gina Engel's murder."

She could leave him. It was just a bigger version of leaving Matthew. If he couldn't give her what she needed, she could leave him, and do so without being destroyed. They'd changed her. This certainty of hers had come from them.

But if he *could* give her this, there'd be a wedding, she'd have a husband, there'd be a life, a glorious life. Because it wouldn't be a broken bone that had been incorrectly set, but something rebuilt, stronger than before.

There was nothing. He was still. He was breathing.

She opened her eyes and he was weeping.

She was skeptical. He wept all the time. But he was scared. This was not something she'd seen before.

He put his cup and saucer down. His fingers tapped against his knees. "I have things to tell you," he said.

Her anxiety elbowed aside the comedy of the line. She waited, watching. Watching was a way to learn. Surely the face of the man she loved more than she'd loved anyone would be eloquent.

He seemed to know not to touch her. He kept his hands laced. He did not hang his head, did not look at his feet. He looked at her. She did not know whether to interpret this as a good sign or a bad one. Sincerity or performance?

"I met her in May of seventy-six," he said.

"Who?" she said.

"Gina," he said.

She nodded. Okay, she thought. So he knew her.

"Okay," he said. "Don't interrupt. I just talk."

She leaned back to reassure him that he wouldn't be hearing another sound out of her.

"I met her at the bar. At our bar," he said. He looked past her to the bookcases. "I'm sorry about that part."

"Me too," Lily said.

The apartment was growing darker. Neither of them moved to turn on the lights.

"What else are you sorry about?" Lily asked.

He looked pained. How, his expression seemed to say, had he become the kind of man who caused damage to the people he cared about most?

"What am I not sorry about?" he said, stirring his tea with his middle finger.

He was not asking for sympathy. His upset seemed genuine. She loved him. It made her want to pursue her questions more, not less. She owed them that. The two of them were worth at least that kind of rigorous care.

"Where do I begin?" he asked.

"The murder part," Lily said. She was remarkably calm.

So was he. "I didn't kill her," he said.

She studied him. There were no bells going off inside her either way, but nothing about her insides had relaxed. How would they ever get out from under all of this?

"But," he said. "It's complicated."

He was beating on her heart with the heels of his hands.

He seemed to have lost his train of thought.

"What?" she said. "What? You didn't kill her, but? Was there a problem because of your drinking?" she prompted.

"There's always a problem," he said like a disappointed parent.

She waited, trying not to be impatient with matter-of-fact statements and sweeping generalities.

He took a breath. "There was a disagreement," he said.

The passive voice bothered her. "Between whom?" she asked.

He glanced at her as if to say that if she kept asking questions like this, he'd never say what he had to.

"It was idiotic," he said. "*I* am idiotic. It was about shirts." He shrugged, embarrassed.

Lily looked at him.

"She was supposed to pick up my shirts at the cleaner, and she didn't, so I didn't have a clean shirt, and I had to be somewhere, I forget where now, and—" He looked to the ceiling. "And. So." He shrugged again. "So there was a disagreement."

"Are you using the right word?" Lily asked.

He looked at her quizzically, as if it were entirely plausible that he was using all the wrong words.

"Disagreement," she said. "Do you mean *disagreement?*"

He was unsure. "I think it's right," he said. "One person thinks one thing, the other thinks something else."

"I'm just trying to hurry this narrative along a bit," she said. "Are you talking about thoughts or actions?"

He was miserable. She couldn't imagine feeling as she had felt the other day in his hallway, pressed up against the wall. She couldn't believe she had thought about running for the door. She couldn't imagine him committing murder.

"I hit her," he said. "Very hard." He raised his arm across his face, the back of his hand facing Lily. "Like this," he said. He swung his arm. The air moved across Lily's face.

"And like this," he said. He cupped his hand and swung it back through the space between them.

Backhanded, she thought. Cuffed. Sentences filled her mind like bricks. *She was backhanded. He cuffed her.*

"What did she do?" she asked.

He was crying. "She was so small," he said. "What could she do? I am big." He squeezed his eyes shut and took breaths through his mouth as if he'd been jogging for miles. "I don't like to think about it," he said.

"Neither do I," said Lily.

"I wish it were a different story," he said.

"So do I," she said.

He opened his eyes, as if she'd hit on the heart of the issue. "You see why I was scared," he said.

Lily wasn't sure what the heart of this issue was.

"Even now," he said. "You're thinking you'll have to leave."

He was right. She *was*. It wasn't the only thing she was thinking.

She held up the card with the photo of the rice bowl. "What about this?" she said.

"I wrote them to Gina's son. I wanted him to feel not so alone." He shrugged. "I liked him," he added.

"Why didn't you sign your name?" she asked.

"I didn't want to be connected with his mother," he said. "Selfish. I know."

They sat there with the card between them.

"Without you, I cannot live," he said.

She had been thinking the same thing. She'd survive, but living a life where every day she woke up lucky and charmed, as if beneath everything she did or said, she could feel her blood running its roundabout course? That life she wouldn't have without him.

She took his hand. He began crying again. She was crying too. It was like after they made love, when they were astonished, when tears were the only available response and turned out to be appropriate.

"I believe you didn't do it," she said.

He kissed her hand, knuckle by knuckle. He kissed the spot on her third finger where her wedding ring would go.

It was not just his kisses. She was telling the truth: she didn't believe it. Though he was capable of it.

She was going to marry a man capable of murder. It was sitting at the edge of a cliff, feet dangling. It was swinging so high, your bottom lifted from the seat. It was the drastic dip of an airplane before it righted itself.

It was nothing she'd ever dreamed of. It was nothing she'd known to ask for. It was something she wouldn't give up.

III

September 1988

ten

Louise Carpanetti had cancer. Her young doctor had told her that morning in a dimly lit room in the clinic. *The Cancer,* her mother and aunts used to call it, as if referring to the president. Because the doctor had a soft spot for Italian grandmother types, at first he'd told her a year, maybe more. He'd also told her about treatment: radiation, chemotherapy, surgery. Louise was seventy-three, a widow for forty-four years, a mother for fifty-five, a smoker for fifty-eight. Her gut told her it would be much less than a year, with or without treatment. When pressed, the kind young doctor had agreed. Well. She'd lived most of her life expecting the worst. She wasn't worried about herself. She was worried about her son.

She got off the M104 bus on 102nd and Broadway, taking the deep steps carefully. She thanked the driver, checked the latch on her good handbag, and headed west to the apartment on the fifth floor where she lived alone with her son.

It was an Indian summer day. School started the next day, and the neighborhood kids ran a little wilder than usual, fighting what they knew was coming. The street was swarming with strollers, mothers, and nannies. Dirty, gritty Broadway was getting cleaner and cleaner. When Louise and her Elia had moved into this apartment, you never saw strollers like these—fancy, with sunshades. You never saw nannies. The stores on Broadway were tiny things in a row. A dairy grocery next to a bakery next to a meat market next to a Chinese food shop. Tall apartment buildings next to five-story walk-ups. Apartment hotels with single-room occupants. Now, she could be anywhere. What difference did it make that sixteen-year-old Louise had sneaked out of her parents' house in Gravesend to join Jewish Elia on the Upper West Side? Her Catholic mother and father and her five Catholic younger brothers hadn't spoken to her again. She saw them at funerals, where her father would give her a small nod and her mother would look at her and weep. Now, her parents, Elia's parents, and Elia were all dead, her brothers moved to suburbs she'd never seen. After the war, after Elia died, she'd thought about leaving the city. But what for? Big beautiful houses with nobody there. If you wanted to take a walk, you walked with a squirrel. Everyone lived everywhere. She didn't feel one way or another about the change. It was change. What could you do?

The breeze off the river lifted the scarf on her hair. She had to go to the parlor. Her hair was a mess. She would lose her hair, she thought, closing her eyes for a minute. The breeze still smelled like summer, like heat and day-old food, sweaty children, and metal. But there were leaves on the ground already, more turning colors above her. Last winter, the movies had come to their block. Trailers and cables, people and chairs everywhere. No one famous. No one from her magazines. But the whole block, transformed out of winter. The bare limbs of trees dressed in leaves, like her mother's lacework in orange and gold.

She was glad for the red light at West End. A chance to catch her breath. She read the flyers on the light post. Lost cats, English classes, guitar lessons, roommates wanted. So much need, so many desires. She felt embarrassed reading about them.

Her son was sitting in a folding chair outside their building. He was wearing his gray sweatpants, his undershirt, a Yankees cap. Everything about him looked like it needed to be hitched up by the belt loops. The chest hairs over the top of the shirt were gray. He was a middle-aged man. She could see him the way the world saw him—a lost, sad figure. Strangers sometimes looked at him as if looking at a dog she'd assured them didn't bite. An odd mix of Italian and Italian Jew, the deck stacked against him from the beginning. It's not your fault, she wanted to tell him. Your mother loved your father, your father loved her back. A child gets to say nothing about who his parents love, for how long or in what ways.

She reached out and cupped his cheek. He leaned into it and closed his eyes like a cat.

Charlie, the boy from upstairs, was sitting next to him. In front of them, they'd spread out her comforter with the lilac print. On that, in disarray, some of her things. The wooden turtle whose shell lifted to reveal a candy dish. The Japanese glass ball Elia had brought back on his first leave. "Fishing buoys," he'd said, unwrapping it in their living room. "Can you believe how beautiful?" he'd said.

Her nightgowns were spread out as if by a maid. Below them, her knee-highs, toes pointing out like Charlie Chaplin at rest. Over some of the nightgowns, her bras, hooked carefully, stuffed with rolled-up socks.

The sign, written on a small green chalkboard in Charlie's ten-year-old handwriting, said: MAKE US AN OFFER WE CAN'T REFUSE.

Michael was taken with the old Godfather movies. "We're Sicilian; they're Sicilian," he'd tried to explain to her. "His name is Michael. My name is Michael."

"Half Sicilian," she always said. "Your father's family was from Ferrara."

"*You're* Sicilian," he would say.

Something about the movies felt vaguely insulting, and she thought that maybe watching that violence wasn't such a good idea for him, but she kept her opinions to herself. They made him happy. What did it matter what she did or didn't understand?

Here were her underclothes on the sidewalk. She sighed, scanning the items. "Sell anything?" she asked, trying to guess what might be missing.

"Lots," Michael said. He didn't offer specifics. He unzipped the black fanny pack that was hanging from the arm of his chair and held out a handful of ones.

She waved at him. "You keep it," she said. "You did the work."

She could feel the cancer in her lungs. His hands were soft and smooth, nothing like the hands of the men in her family— dockworkers and laborers. His hands were like homemades she'd pressed into shape at her kitchen table.

She wouldn't tell him about the cancer. What good would it do? She'd figure out how to take care of him after she was gone. Then she'd tell him. Change made him nervous. So did loud noises and rooms that were too quiet, fancy clothes, and most grown-ups. He preferred children. He hated doctors and dentists. He hated teachers. She'd moved their living room furniture around once, and when he'd seen it, she'd had to move it back again. Before she told him anything, she wanted to have lots of information to offer.

She lowered herself to the stoop. He was whistling. She never recognized the tune. She leaned forward. "How you doing, Charlie?" she asked the boy. His hair was a rat's nest of dreadlocks. His father was black; his mother was white. They seemed happy, but what did she know?

He smiled at her. "Good, Mrs. C. And you?"

She closed her eyes. Nice boy, she thought. Polite. Too bad about the hair.

the mornings just after waking were the best and the worst part of the day. For a minute the little paws of cancer pressing on her chest were gone. The images of her insides eaten away hadn't yet formed. The sounds of the building and the street below were just sounds.

And then the knowledge returned in a slow march. The nice doctor. The genuine pain in his eyes. The way his fancy wristwatch had beeped and he'd ignored it. She had been glad for him then, was glad for him each morning. She imagined the cancer like a school of those yellow eating machines from the video game Michael liked to play at the Puerto Rican store on the corner.

She would lie in her bed, trying to keep the remembering from infecting everything. It seemed uninterested in her desires.

Then, slowly, the sounds of the children going to school made her nauseous. She had lost three babies after Michael, despite prayer after prayer to Saint Anne. She'd been willing to lose more, but Elia had shook his head, sad and heavy, like a horse, and put up his hand like a crossing guard.

There were the sounds of her neighbors' water rushing

through the pipes, or the heat clanging its way out of the radiators. But the sounds of Michael in the kitchen making his toast, soaking his cereal, pouring his juice terrified her. What would happen? What would happen to him?

Her whole life as a mother had been spent asking this question in one context or another.

She thought of what she could make happen. Lying there in bed, Elia's side of the bed smooth and undisturbed, she made lists in her head. She did calculations with her office-girl mind. She wrote in the air with a fingernail yellow from smoke.

There was enough money for him, a rent-controlled apartment, Elia's life insurance and army pension, her savings from years at Weinberger and Sons, Certified Public Accountants, her pension. What had they ever needed? A roof, some food, furniture built to last, a movie a week. *La miseria,* her mother had called it—a way of life that included malaria, cholera, earthquakes, volcanos, tidal waves. Louise's life was far from that.

Until a few years ago, she'd kept the money in the mattress, like her mother. But she'd finally needed to replace the mattress—it was like sleeping in a hammock—and the office girl in her had won out and she'd gone to the Apple Bank on Seventy-Fourth and Broadway to open a passbook savings account. They were giving away toasters, and she thought the red apple on their sign was festive, a sign of luck. She earned 2.2% interest and put Michael's name under hers on the account so he wouldn't have to pay taxes on it when her time came.

The mattress she'd replaced by calling 1-800-MATTRESS. One hundred dollars, removal included. The two guys looked too skinny to carry anything. She'd never seen skin as dark. Haitian, she guessed, or the Senegalese who sold African things that smelled strange on blankets up and down Broadway. They'd noticed the slit in the mattress.

So money was not the problem. And even she knew that he could do fine on his own. Five years ago, when she'd been in the hospital for gallstones, he'd done fine without her. Maybe better. He hadn't burned the building down. He hadn't bothered the neighbors. He'd even vacuumed and cleaned the kitchen. He had said, though, that another day by himself and he'd go nuts.

So, she'd say to herself, staring at the ceiling, What is the problem then?

That's when she wept, because her mind shut down at the understanding that dying meant leaving her son. Fine, she thought of saying to the cancer. Take me. What does that have to do with him?

She'd weep for a minute and then wipe her eyes roughly. "For God's sake," she'd say, impatient. She'd pinch lightly at her cheeks and pull back the covers to start her day.

She told her best friend, Muriel Yablonsky, from down the block. When their kids were young and they had a rare Saturday or Sunday off from the weekend piecework they did at home, they went to the park. Sometimes they only got as far as Louise's stoop. "Play here," they'd say to Michael and Muriel's twin boys, handing them a piece of chalk and a rubber ball.

Now the twins were grown and living in Jersey, married to blondes Louise couldn't tell apart. Michael still had his toy wooden gun armed with rubber bands, set to discharge those square pieces of oilcloth. Now the old friends had time to sit at

Muriel's kitchen table, smoke cigarettes over cups of coffee slowly growing cold.

Before the war, when Elia thought her girl time was up, he'd send Michael to stand in front of Muriel's windows and yell for her. "Ma! Ma! Pop says come home or he'll give you something to gab about." But Elia was the neighborhood softie, walked to his barbershop on Amsterdam Avenue at quarter of eight every morning, came home at quarter past six every night, handing out candy from his coat both ways. He tipped his hat at neighborhood women and threw pitches for the boys playing in the street. He sighed and commiserated with Mr. Kashner who owned the dairy store on the corner. He was Jewish; people thought he was wise.

When she thought about her life with him, she was astonished to realize how few years it actually covered: thirteen, 1931 to 1944, when the telegram had come. Thirteen out of seventy-three. No time at all, and space enough for a whole life. Her life with him was only part of other lives he'd had: the barbershop, the army, the woman with the Russian accent who'd shown up at the memorial service accompanied by a boy a few years younger than Michael. The boy looked like a miniature Elia. If Louise could see it, everyone else could. But no one had said a thing, then or later. Not when the boy, Nikolai, started showing up on the block, playing with the neighborhood kids, keeping his eye on her. Not when, in his twenties, money coming in from somewhere, dressed in gabardine pants and shirts with French cuffs, he started bringing them things: Prosciutt from Bleeker Street. Rolls from Ratner's. A couple of bucks for Michael. A scarf for Louise. Once, for a few months, a car he said he needed them to watch.

Being around Muriel always reminded Louise that marrying a

Jew didn't mean she was a Jew. And Italian Jew wasn't real Jew. Muriel was a real Jew. Her parents had been Socialists, her father had built row houses in Philadelphia, her mother had written letters and filled out forms for the other Jews who didn't speak English. In the seventies, Muriel had divorced her tailor husband and started dying her hair orange and wearing caftans and dangling wooden earrings. She volunteered as a reading teacher at a school in the Bronx, and invited the kids to her house and used them for her courses at Columbia. She was getting a degree in education. Louise had seen one of the experiments once. It had involved filling water glasses of different shapes to various levels and asking the kids questions about them. Muriel had seemed excited by the answers.

The kettle was whistling. Muriel let it. "Jesus Christ, Louise," she said. "You gotta let the doctors do what they're trained to do."

"The kettle," Louise said. She poked through the bowl of hard candy on Muriel's table, searching for butterscotch.

Muriel poured hot water into the mugs. She was making Louise drink tea. Something herbal from that crazy health food place on Broadway. The tea strainer looked like it was filled with dirt.

"You got coffee?" Louise asked again.

"You're not having coffee," Muriel said.

Louise didn't argue. Both women were hard workers, their households smoothly running machines. But Muriel was better at getting what she wanted by way of announcement. Louise was better by way of endurance.

"Coffee would be good," Louise said.

"Coffee's not good for you," Muriel said.

Louise nodded and shrugged.

Muriel sighed and started filling the percolator.

"What about Michael?" Muriel asked.

Louise admired that say-anything-to-anybody quality, but each time she was witness to it, it took her by surprise, as if one of her elderly aunts had reached over and shoved her.

"He'll be okay," she said.

Muriel was quiet.

"There's money," Louise said. It felt funny to say out loud. It was like hearing her voice on tape. Once, she and Michael had squeezed into a booth in the music store on Amsterdam and made a record to send to Elia in the army. Michael had refused to talk. It was a recording of coaxing broken by long silences. The record had picked up his breathing.

"Maybe Nikolai could help," Muriel said quietly. They hadn't talked about him much. Muriel would look at the new air conditioner in the bedroom window, the Mr. Coffee, the new TV, and neither of them would ever raise the obvious questions.

Louise shrugged. "He doesn't owe us," she said. Nick had left the city a decade ago. Married a China girl and left. It had surprised Louise, but how well had she known him anyway? Sometimes he still sent money, no return address. After he left, Manuel and Tina had come back to the building. Louise didn't know why they'd given up the fancy doorman job Nikolai had gotten them, but she was glad they were back.

"Michael'll be fine," she went on, as if she were talking about being away for a couple of hours.

"Money's not what I meant," Muriel said.

Louise turned the butterscotch around inside her mouth. It was the taste of special treats and sickness all at once.

"What's he gonna do without you?" Muriel asked.

The coffee was percolating in the top of the coffeemaker. Louise tried to concentrate on it. She waved away the smoke from her cigarette. "What he's always done."

Muriel gave her her social worker look. "Can he do that without you?"

Louise shrugged. She didn't say anything. What did it matter what he could or couldn't do? Whoever said anyone was getting a choice?

thursday, she took Michael to Coney Island.

"The beach?" he said, looking to the ceiling as if checking the weather.

"The beach," she said. "We'll take a walk."

"It's a long ride," he said.

"Yes, it is," she said.

On the way to the subway station, she handed him the Baggie with the four tokens. "Take two out for now," she said. "Put the others in your pocket for coming home."

He did as he was told, then slipped his hand into hers.

They had to change twice. By the last stop in Manhattan, the subway was empty except for a Puerto Rican teenager at the end of the car. She looped her handbag strap around her wrist.

"No one's going to the beach," Michael said.

"We're going," Louise answered. "Maybe he's going," she added.

"I don't like the beach," her son said. He was still holding her hand.

"*I* like it," she said. "It's where I met your father."

"I know," he said.

And then it was too loud to talk. She concentrated on where she was.

She'd been lying on a blanket with her three girlfriends, getting as much warmth from each other as from the sun. Rosa, Allegrina, and Cookie. When one of them turned, they all turned.

Louise looked like their kid sister. Short and thin, her chest flat, her hair frizzy and wild. Worse on the beach.

Each neighborhood had its own bay, a stretch about two blocks wide. Bay 10 was Italian. The Jewish kids walked over from the other side of Ocean Parkway to Bay 7. Bays 8 and 9 were empty. Two bays completely empty.

Elia had crossed the empty strip of beach and stood in front of their blanket, his shadow across their legs. His black hair was slicked back. His eyes were olive green. He was completely dry but looked as if he'd just stepped from the water. She'd almost expected him to stretch and sigh.

He'd smiled at all of them with good teeth. "Ladies," he'd said.

Cookie had sat up and struck her pinup pose. "Gentleman," she'd said.

"Come take a walk with me," he'd said to Louise, holding out a hand with thin fingers tapering to well-kept nails.

So they'd walked down the beach, Louise careful to keep their arms from touching. He bought himself a hot dog, French fries, and a large ear of roasted corn. He offered her whatever she wanted, but she said no. It didn't seem right to have a stranger spend twenty-five cents on her. He'd wiped his fingers on his thighs. Now she remembered almost nothing about their conversation. Had she talked at all? But at the end of the boardwalk, he'd buried his nose in her hair. She remembered that. She'd wished for Allegrina's silky straight hair, and she had to keep herself from pulling away.

"You smell like something," he said.

"Sorry," she said.

He took her hand and cupped it, upside down, in his.

She resisted the unlikely impulse to snap the waistband of his bathing trunks.

Later, his reputation as a solid, reliable, decent man would be so convincing that she'd be surprised when she remembered that their life had begun that way. Maybe that's why the Russian woman at the service hadn't stopped her short. Maybe there'd been women like that one all along. Maybe he hadn't kept secrets from her. Maybe she'd done that to herself.

A stop away from Ocean Parkway, she felt a disturbance in the air, as if someone had opened the doors while the train was still moving. She checked. Michael was there. He was looking at the teenager, whose chin was against his chest. The boy seemed to be asleep.

"You see that?" Michael said.

Louise had that feeling that she sometimes got with her son, that she was being addressed by a stranger.

"No," she said. She didn't know if she had the energy for this.

He sat up a little straighter and rested his hands on his knees. "That guy's looking at me."

She weighed her options. "Looks like he's sleeping," she said.

Michael snorted. She was being thick. It was his cross to bear. "He's not sleeping," he said. "He's got his eye on me." He shifted his weight from side to side, gripped the edge of the plastic seat, and called the boy a name under his breath.

Cursing was never a good sign.

She put a hand on his wide shoulder and rubbed slow circles. "Our stop next," she said, but it was like she wasn't there.

"Hey," he called out. "Hey, fella." He said "fella" like the two guys in the building who had moved in last year. Roommates, they said.

It took the teenager a minute to realize Michael was talking to him.

"I see you," Michael said.

"Michael Ermanno," Louise said. Sometimes that worked.

The teenager was still slumped in his chair, but now he was awake, watching Michael. He tucked his hand in the waistband of his jeans and left it there. "Can I help you?" he asked.

"No," Michael said, rising. "You can't."

For Louise, it was like trying to stand in open water too far from shore. Michael's episodes were like waves lifting her off her feet. The effect was cumulative. Enough waves and you felt like your whole life was open water.

This episode went the way they all did. Maybe better than some. Michael did his stamping and snorting. The boy did his. Louise made her usual attempts to calm things down. Michael had his reactions. She landed almost softly on one of the seats, a railing nearby to hold on to. The boy watched her fall and stepped back. The doors opened at Ocean Parkway, and he left.

They watched him disappear down the stairs, and then the doors closed.

She patted the seat next to her and told Michael to sit down, and he did, his shoulder rocking against hers as the train started to move back the way they had come.

. . .

She'd known about the cancer for close to three weeks. Fall had arrived for good. Children were resigned to their school-year routine and didn't argue with their parents on the way up the block in the morning. They came running down the hill in the afternoon, backpacks dangling by a strap and hitting the sidewalk like the cans and shoes behind a newlyweds' car. "Stay where I can see you," the mothers called out. "Stop at the corner." The fancy new mothers in the neighborhood sent their children to progressive private schools and donated to all the right things, but the longtime residents made them nervous. Ashamed, they smiled at the black teenage fathers sitting on their stoops with their toddlers and the loud, unintelligible music coming from their boom boxes. They nodded to the Dominican handymen playing dominos on card tables at the top of the basement stairs. But they were ready to throw themselves on their children in an instant. They were Secret Service agents, one hand on the hood of the president's car.

Louise saw all this from her window. She sat sidesaddle on the radiator cover, her back against the lower sash. Though the air was chilly, the window was open wide enough for her hand and the cigarette in it, the smoke moving in the air like breath.

The *Daily News* and the *Post* were on the kitchen table. Page one of the *Post* said NABBED! over a photo of a man getting into a car. She didn't read the story. On page three of the *News*, there was a small article with no byline. EX-HUSBAND NABBED AFTER TWELVE YEARS.

When Louise got her second cup of coffee and sat to read, she almost didn't make it to page three, but she forced herself for the sake of routine. He had lied. He'd been in New York that day. His second ex-wife said that he and Gina had been "negotiating a new financial arrangement." There had been some disagreement. He was going to New York to work it out. Someone had seen him sitting in a car around the corner from the building. Someone else had seen him on the stairs. There were flight records. The defense said it was nothing but circumstantial evidence. The DA said the evidence might be circumstantial, but it was strong circumstantial evidence. Evidence was evidence.

Louise's old suspicions came spilling out inside of her. The old arguments surfaced. It was crazy. Whatever Michael was, he wasn't a murderer. *Was* it crazy? He'd been down Gina and Steven's that night, but he was always down Gina and Steven's on Tuesday nights. They watched the nature shows together. He hadn't come home covered in blood. But still, for two days he'd been someone she hadn't recognized. For two days, someone she didn't know.

She'd thought about telling someone then. The police had interviewed both of them late that night, and again a few days later. Michael hadn't seemed suspicious to them. He'd said he'd gone down for his usual Tuesday night thing, but no one had been home, so he'd gone to the store instead. He'd hung out there, and then he'd come home.

What was she going to tell the police? That he hadn't turned on the TV or the radio in two days? That he'd skipped his daily dominoes game in the park? That he ate standing up? Avoided his favorite chair? Took a shower three times in one day? These were things that meant he was a murderer? She'd been stabbed and there wasn't a spot of blood on his clothes. But he'd come home in his undershirt, without his top shirt. It wasn't the first time he'd come home missing something, no idea where it had gone, but still.

He'd avoided his bed. For two nights, she'd found him in the living room, lying on his back between the couch and the wall. He'd pulled the couch away from the wall to make space for himself. She'd sat in the armchair across the room from him both nights, neither of them saying a word about it the following mornings.

But even that was just that: strange boys did strange things. It wasn't anything like proof.

The police were more interested in Louise, anyway. They told her that Gina's phone records had indicated a call to her right around the time of death.

Louise's skin had tingled. She'd almost laughed. Yes, she'd said, she'd gotten a call, but she hadn't known who it was. The sounds had been incoherent. A crank, she'd thought. And they'd believed her.

She hadn't recognized the voice, but she'd recognized that somebody was in horrible pain, and she hadn't done anything.

So she hadn't told anyone about Michael, not even Muriel. Instead, she'd played cop. She checked her knife drawer. She poked around Michael's room when he was out. She asked him questions she felt ridiculous asking, checking the story he'd told the police. She asked the Puerto Ricans if Michael had been any trouble that night in the store. He had been there and he hadn't been any trouble, but they couldn't remember exactly when or for how long.

And then she put her suspicions away. Sometimes, when her guard was down, the drawer slid open, all her arguments and evidence laid out there in neat little rows. When that happened, she worried them in tight, hushed ways, and then shut the drawer again.

So the cancer and the article were punishment. She'd always known that where she failed, God would sort it out. And now here He was, telling her to set things right in the time she had left.

She couldn't let someone else suffer for something she thought Michael might've done.

She'd stood by and watched the boy lose his mother. She'd told herself she hadn't known it was Gina on the other end of the phone. The call had lasted half a minute. The woman had said Louise's name, as if all the inhuman sounds before that had been the sounds of her name making its way out.

The woman had said her name. Had she *really* not recognized the voice? It was *her name*. How many people did she know? And why had she been calling?

It was amazing what a person could come up against in herself and still keep going. Shop, mail letters, do laundry, cook dinner. A million times she'd told herself that if she had it to do over again, she'd do things differently. She hadn't really wanted the chance, but here it was. Now, twelve years later, could she really stand by and watch him lose his father?

For all she knew, it *was* the father.

She tore the page from the paper, folded it, and put it in her purse. And then she sat back at the window and watched for her son to come whistling down the block.

eleven

Louise had no idea where the New York County Supreme Court was, and the paper said the arraignment was tomorrow. Downtown, she guessed, at the base of the Brooklyn Bridge, with all those buildings crammed together like steerage passengers. Government made her nervous. Government buildings were no exception. She didn't even like going to the post office, though at least at the Gravesend branch of her childhood, all the workers had spoken Italian. Up here, those men and women in their wash-and-wear uniforms behind their oversized counters looked at her with her incorrectly addressed envelopes and her wrong denomination stamps and made faces. She tried not to make trouble for them. She tried to be a good customer, a familiar customer, but she knew she wasn't either. Still, she always thought, staring down whoever was behind the counter waiting for her to gather herself, what gave them the right to point out what she already knew about herself?

Muriel would know where it was, but Muriel would have questions. So who else was there to ask? It used to be her parents and her brothers. Then Elia. One by one she'd watched each of them leave, or had shown them the door, and now she found herself with no one but Michael. And since the murder, she hadn't been big on questions.

She stood up and told herself to quit the sorry-for-herself stuff. If she had a question, she should find an answer.

She got the phone book from on top of the fridge. New York County Supreme Court, 100 Centre Street.

he'd swallowed the thimble when he was two. She'd been doing her weekend piecework, the cloth she was edging on her sewing table by the front window, her scissors, thread, and thimble on top of the pile. He'd been marching around after a rubber ball. She'd gone to the kitchen to start the sauce and she'd talked to him from there, giving him her usual running commentary. She couldn't have been gone longer than five minutes. When she got back to the front room, he was sitting on the floor.

She'd fished the thimble out quickly, two fingers down his slippery throat, and had talked to him the whole time. Afterward, holding him in her lap there on the floor, his raspy sobs quieting, she'd kept talking, and she'd understood that she was watching herself take two directions at once. There was what had happened just now, a story between mother and son, and there was what she'd tell Elia: another, different story between husband and wife. She'd pinned an amulet shaped in the form of horns to the inside of his undershirt. The same one her mother had pinned to her to ensure them safety on the long voyage from Naples to New York. She hadn't known it would be so easy to keep secrets from a husband, even one she loved as much as Elia.

So, later still, when Michael started to seem a bit slow, a little awkward at socializing, easy to anger, stubborn, she thought of the thimble, but didn't share those thoughts with Elia, one secret having paved the way for others. And really, after it was clear that Michael wasn't just a little slow, a little awkward, after he'd dropped out of high school, lost or quit four jobs in two months, cost her much more than she had to spare to pay for all the breakable objects he took his frustrations out on, after all that, *why* didn't seem to matter so much.

So she could believe it was that small piece of metal; Elia, the coddling; Muriel, the drinking he'd done as a teenager; and Father Camini could say it was God's will. What mattered was that something in his head didn't work right. It didn't seem like something that could be repaired. It was something to bear.

He tried the army, but that didn't work out. He worked as a janitor at a private school, a night watchman for a youth center, a delivery boy for the grocery around the corner. He drank. Those boys from East Harlem and Monte Carmelo who she never trusted took him off in their cars, bringing him back drunk and confused. Sometimes the police brought him back, always with embarrassed low voices and sympathy in their eyes.

Sometimes there was trouble. Most of the time there wasn't. Most of the time, for the last several years, their life had been planning for the next meal, reading the papers, watching the TV. They concentrated on not getting in each other's way. The TV and the radio were always on. Both at once. But they still listened for each other's sounds in the apartment, those sounds offering more comfort than anything else.

She told Michael she was going over Muriel's. He was sitting in the window. He said what he always said. "Have a good time. Don't talk about me."

He seemed good.

She took the one train to Franklin. 100 Centre Street was three blocks south of Canal. She'd looked it up on her street map so she wouldn't have to consult it down there. An old woman on a street corner with an open map? You might as well just hand over your bag.

There were steps, and by the time she made it into the lobby, she was out of breath. She paused. People pushed their way around her. She hadn't expected so many people. Most of them were black. She found a bench against a wall. In front of her, there was a circular desk with two tall empty chairs behind it. Cops in uniforms milled around the lobby. There was an impossibly small newsstand. A cafeteria, the source of the unpleasant smells. Behind the desk, telephones. Above it, a black ball of a clock with Roman numerals in gold. It said three-twenty. Louise checked her watch. It was ten after nine.

The ceilings were high. The floors were granite. The sounds were echoey and lost, like she was in a tunnel. Everyone was moving fast and knew where they were going. What was she doing here? Replaying an old argument about what her son was or wasn't capable of.

She fished a dime out of her change purse and called home.

He always said hello like he was the happiest guy in the world.

"You're calling me from Muriel's?" he said.

"Why not?" she said.

"It's loud," he said.

"TV," she said. "We're talking about you," she said.

"Yeah, right," he said. "Whaddya saying?"

"What are we not saying," she said.

An officer came out of the men's room and headed behind the information desk. There was a line of unhappy women waiting for him. He took his time settling in.

"So you're okay?" she said.

"You were here five minutes ago," he said. "I'm the same."

"Well, that's good," she said.

They were quiet.

"What's Muriel doing?" he asked.

"I don't know. She's in the bathroom," she said.

"Ma?" he said.

"Yeah?" she said.

"You coming home soon?"

"Yeah," she said. "Couple hours. Want me to make pizza?"

"Whatever you want," he said.

"Okay then," she said. She saw a green sign pointing down the hallway she had just been sitting in: Arraignments.

"Okay," he said.

"See you soon," she said.

"Yeah," he said. "Okeydokey."

It was one of those things he said that made him sound eight or a hundred and two.

She hung up. She should've stayed on a little longer, gotten her dime's worth.

She headed down the hallway. At a set of double doors a woman with a baby pushed by her. A few typed pages were taped up next to the doors. Louise got out her glasses and waited for the teenager in front of her to finish looking at the list. Four columns: *Calendar, L, Case #, Defendant's Name.* Under *Calendar* was a long column of two-digit numbers preceded by *Part.* Under *L* was *AA6,* then a list of numbers starting with one. A small group piled behind her, trying to see the list. She found herself being pushed through the double doors. AR1, the sign said.

The room was like the waiting room of a train station. The benches were filled with people. No one looked like they were together. There were eight or ten people behind the low wall. The only one Louise could identify was the judge. To the left of the judge, in two rows of benches facing the wall, grim-looking young men sat waiting.

There were letters reading IN GOD WE TRUST behind the judge. There were what looked like bullet holes in the wall below it. She strained to hear. The whole place was making her anxious.

She went back out to the circular desk and handed the officer the newspaper article.

"Eleventh floor," he said. "Room eleven hundred, Part seventy."

She had no idea what "Part seventy" meant.

"Is there a time?" she asked.

"No," he said. "You just gotta wait."

She thanked him. He barely acknowledged her.

The elevator was jammed. Everyone was sweaty. The doors opened onto another hallway lined with more benches. More teenage mothers with tiny babies. Toddlers climbed onto benches and marched the length of them. There was a long line for the one pay phone.

She settled onto another bench. She kept her coat and scarf on. She put her handbag on her lap and checked her wristwatch, a gift from Nick. Nine thirty. Here she was, waiting for an arraignment at nine thirty in the morning. What did she think she would do in that courtroom?

She imagined telling someone that in fifty-plus years of being his mother, she'd never seen him act like he'd acted in those two days after the murder. That in the year after Steven moved away, Michael had written letter after letter to him. He had given them all to Louise to mail, and she had walked to the post office and mailed them, unread.

He wasn't a murderer.

Her heart was going nuts. She took some deep breaths. What did she really know? This wasn't knowledge. This was the opposite of knowledge.

For now, she'd wait. Soon, she'd go into Room 1100, and then she'd see what she would see. What else could she do?

At first, she got excited when he told her he liked a girl. He had his eye on someone. There was someone he thought she'd really like. She couldn't remember when that gave way to a clutch in the stomach, a knowledge of what was coming. When had she gone from asking when he was going to bring this someone by, to asking him nothing, trying not to pop his bubble but to deflate it slowly?

Since the murder, he hadn't mentioned anyone. She didn't know whether that was a good sign or a bad one.

In his bottom drawer there were girlie magazines. There'd been the time when those East Harlem boys had come by to pick him up, a small giggly girl in the backseat, the whole car throbbing with music.

He wasn't going to get a girlfriend, have a wife. At some point he must've understood that too. Who knew what his sadness and anger felt like? All she knew was that he deserved to feel both.

In Room 1100 a woman standing at the table near the empty jury box read lazily from a big stack of papers. People came and went. Louise sat in the second row, and still it was impossible to hear what they were saying. There were fewer people on the benches than there'd been downstairs. More single women and their babies.

Giant light fixtures that looked like upside-down tables hung from the tall ceilings.

She was worried she was sitting in the wrong seat.

She hadn't been to confession in twelve years. She was surprised at how easily she'd slipped out of the habit. Her mother had gone to mass every day, finding time for it between the garment shop and the hours at home making artificial flowers. Her father went only on the big days—Christmas, Easter, first communions, confirmations. And sometimes not even then. He worked on the docks even longer hours than her mother, leaving so early, coming home so late, that sometimes Louise wouldn't see him for days, and when she did see him, coming out of the bath-room, sinking into his chair, rising from his bed, it often took her a second to recognize him. Like seeing a child before and after a growth spurt. She wished for her mother and father on the bench next to her. Her mother and father before she'd become the biggest disappointment of their lives, before she'd been the cause of so much suffering. Running away with Elia had been the right decision, but still, at seventy-three, she wished for parents.

The judge was a lady. Louise strained to hear. "Part sixty-two," the judge said. "Ten twenty." The judge put her hands up to stop the negotiating. "Wait a minute," she said to the lawyer present-ing. She stared at a man standing by the front row of benches. "Mr. Sere," she said, "have a seat."

The last few weeks, food hadn't been so interesting. She un-wrapped a cracker from her bag. An officer appeared out of nowhere, touched her on the arm, and pointed at the signs on the low wall. FRONT ROW FOR ATTORNEYS AND POLICE OFFICERS ONLY. NO FOOD OR BEVERAGE IN COURTROOM. NO READING OF NEWSPA-PERS IN COURTROOM. THANK YOU.

She blushed, avoiding the eyes of a man across the aisle.

Everywhere she went, she was wrong. Why couldn't life be easier?

But there, in the front row of seats, to the far left, was the boy. Not a boy anymore. Tall, with that same hair.

His mother always had big plans, compensating maybe for hav-ing no father around. But then she'd lose interest, and all the birthday parties turned into the chaos of ten or fifteen boys run-ning up and down the building's stairs with toy guns or slingshots, jumping the last two or three stairs in one leap, flipping like acrobats over the banisters. "Sorry," they always said, disappearing down the next flight. "Sor-ry."

She got up to find a water fountain. She was dizzier. She sat back down and rested her head on the bench in front of her. She could see divots in the wood.

When Michael was a child, she rarely let him touch anything in the city. It was the thing she remembered being told most as a child, *Non toccare.* He took to walking stiffly, his arms glued to his sides.

The man across the aisle asked if he could help. She sat up. She was fine, she told him. It was stuffy in here.

Steven was regarding her from the front row. Blankness gave way to mild confusion. He held up a finger as if pointing her out of a lineup in his mind. He turned the finger into a small wave.

She nodded at him, and then made her way back out the double doors.

In a taxi, she sat back against the black plastic seats and smelled their smell. A cab, she thought. All this money, just to go home.

from his spot in the window, Michael saw her get out of the taxi. He opened the window and stuck his head out. "What's wrong?" he said.

She looked up to give him a wave. It made her dizzier.

"I'm coming down," he said. "Stay there."

She lowered herself onto the stoop and tilted to rest against the stone balustrade. It was even dirtier than the bench in the courtroom. She was resting on anything. She barely recognized herself.

Michael was next to her.

"You took a cab from Muriel's?" he asked.

She shushed him with a raised hand. "I'll explain later," she said.

"You don't look so good," he said.

"That's very nice," she said.

"What happened?" he asked again.

She patted him on the leg. He'd come down in his shorts, with no shoes. The undershirt he'd slept in, the small gold cross she'd given him years ago tucked into it.

He was always next to her.

"I'll tell you later," she said. "Nothing serious. Help me get inside."

"Tell me now," he said, helping her to her feet. His hands were strong and made her think that where they'd ended up had been a big mistake. If they just had the chance to go back, she could do things differently; he could do things differently. Each of them could have the life they should've.

Gina had asked them to feed the cat. That's how they met. They were going away for a few days and needed someone to bring in the mail, feed the cat, water the plants. Gina thought maybe Michael would be interested; she'd heard around the building that he did that kind of thing.

The baby boy was sober but had a solidity to him that Louise recognized from some of her male relatives. Here I am, and here I'm staying. Later, she found out he'd been premature, had spent nearly two months in the hospital, his mother unable to touch him except through the thick rubber gloves on the incubator. Four months after bringing him home, the father had walked out.

"And now," Gina had said, the day they'd met, "here we are."

"What about your family?" Louise had asked.

Gina had smiled. She had a nice smile.

"I'm Italian," she said. "The only daughter. He's Jewish." She shrugged just like Louise would've. "It wasn't what my parents had in mind."

Louise had held a palm up to indicate that there wasn't a thing about what Italian families had in mind for their only daughters that she didn't know.

So there they were. Almost friends. And there Gina had come a few weeks later, up one flight of back stairs to knock on their door and hand Michael the key to her place.

It had been strange to be in someone's apartment without the someone. While Michael had watered and fed, she'd walked around the four rooms resisting the urge to tidy up. The hallway was lined with framed snapshots of different men. She recognized one or two of them. Men she'd seen coming or going with Gina. A wall of photos of former boyfriends was odd. Was it brashness?

She took in the view from the windows. Same as hers, one story down. In the fridge, blue cheese, grapes, sour cream, yogurt, a Sara Lee pound cake, a rack of eggs. On the counter, a jar of ground coffee, one of those fancy cheese slicers, an open container of olives, and a pack of cigarettes. Cutting knives stuck to a strip of magnet. One wall was covered in cork. Photos of baby

Steven. Emergency numbers. Telephone numbers on scraps of paper. Job listings from the newspaper circled in red.

Michael came in to refill the plastic watering can. He was being careful. He was taking his time.

In Gina's bedroom she stood there while he watered the two spider plants and the jade in the window. The hanging spider plants dripped. He caught the excess water by holding his T-shirt out.

Her bed was unmade and covered with throw pillows in purples and oranges and greens. The bottom of the sheets was untucked, as if Gina had spent the night kicking. A nightie was spread over the armchair in the corner. Socks. A bra.

Michael seemed to be concentrating on the plants. "Come on," she said. "We gotta get back."

"Why?" he asked.

He wasn't being wise, but she was impatient with him. "Because we don't live here," she said.

He said he was working, in a way that stressed all her nagging about getting a job, all her disappointment when he'd lost yet another one, all her questions about what he was going to do today, when he was going to get off his rear and get motivated. He knew she prayed for him. He knew when she closed the door to her room for her naps that sometimes she was crying. He knew that sometimes it was over him.

So she went to the kitchen and got one of Gina's cigarettes, lit it, pulled a chair to the window, and thought about that ride Elia had taken her on for their second, secret date. She thought about the Willie's Frozen Custard booth with its corner awnings studded with white bulbs.

In Gina Engel's apartment, she felt something like she'd felt on those secret dates: a deep roller-coaster plunge of a feeling that stopped her cold and left her charged up and fierce, someone she hadn't known she was.

Page three of the *News*: Benjamin Engel had pleaded not guilty to one count of manslaughter in the first degree and one count of sexual assault. No bail. He'd been remanded to Riker's Island. The trial had been set for three weeks from the day before.

The defense attorney was a big shot. He was being assisted by a young member of his firm, a distant acquaintance of Mr. Engel and his son: Samantha Cook.

Louise got the phone book, looked up her number, and wrote it down on the pad by the phone with a pen whose ink was running out.

And then she called. She dialed; it rang. The secretary answered. A long list of names, none of them Cook.

Michael came into the room. "Whaddya doing?" he asked.

Louise put her finger to the plunger and replaced the handset. "Checking the time."

"Something wrong with your watch?" he said.

She shook her head, stood, and wiped her hands on her housecoat. "Wanna make manicott?" she asked.

He shrugged. "Not really," he said. "I'll eat them," he added, as if that might make her feel better.

"You all right?" he asked.

She patted her hair into place. "Why? I don't look all right?"

"You look good," he said. "I don't know. Things seem off around here."

"You're the only thing off around here," she said, then felt like kicking herself. His eyes were doing that flashy thing they did. Like she could see his brain doing its unhappy things.

"I'm going out," he said.

"You don't have to," she said.

He pulled his sweatpants up. "Me and Charlie got stuff to do."

She was worn out so she let him go, managing a "come back soon" before the door shut.

The nausea was back. It had never really left. This morning, there had been more coughing, more blood in tissues stuffed to the bottom of the kitchen garbage pail.

What did she think? One day she'd be gone and Michael wouldn't even notice?

What did it matter what she did with her last days? Either way, she was dying. What did she have to tell Samantha Cook? Maybes and might-haves. An old lady's hunches.

She knew while she was thinking all this that she believed the opposite. It was because she was dying that what she did mattered so much.

And who'd encouraged Michael to get to know that mother and her son? To do errands for them, to take Steven to the park and watch him after school?

Who'd gotten warmth and pleasure from that apartment one floor down, that life that seemed so much like it could've been hers? If she'd been born thirty years later, or had a different kind of son. Or been a different kind of mother. She knew it sometimes seemed like Gina was making the wrong decisions, but all that independence, all that aggressive health, and that sweet, sweet boy.

So what if she'd wanted what someone else had? Who didn't? Who was happy with what God had dished out for them?

At the end of the day, there was just her and Michael. Whatever she had or hadn't done had been for him. She wouldn't have known how to live any other way.

And if she'd been sure that it had been Michael, would she have done anything different? Would she have turned in her own child? How could a mother do that? How could a mother not? If she knew her child took a mother away from another boy, how could she not?

twelve

She'd lost seven pounds in the last week. She weighed less than she'd weighed as a teenager. Her favorite foods made her gag. She left wide wet spots on the sofa.

She saw him from her window on a Saturday, two weeks before the trial. There he was, tall and thin like his father.

Michael was playing video games with Charlie at the Puerto Ricans' store. She didn't like the idea of Michael seeing him.

He was sitting on the stoop across the street, his knees up, his hands between them. He looked like he'd been there his whole life. Regulars walked past without noticing him.

He was dressed nice. He still had the bangs in his eyes like he was saving you from having to look at him.

He watched customers come and go from the drug dealer's apartment on the corner.

How long was he going to sit there? Michael wasn't going to stay at the store forever.

He watched dogwalkers and joggers, old ladies with shopping carts filled with laundry. Manuel and the other supers playing dominoes on overturned boxes. Louise watched with him.

He saw Michael before she did. Michael and Charlie were laughing and drinking Slushies, their lips stained red. Michael had a Charleston Chew sticking out of his front pocket. As they headed up their stoop, she had all three boys in sight at once. This was what heaven would be like—a view of everyone she'd ever known, milling around on the block.

Steven watched them go in. He stood and took a few steps into the street. She stood too and backed away from the window. He looked up at his old windows. The girls who lived there now were college students, unfriendly, a little too wild, in the dark about what had happened there all those years ago. The landlord had had to strip the floors.

She could hear Michael outside the door—his keys, his good-byes to Charlie.

Here the boy was, grown, aged, some things changed, some things not. What could be traced to losing a mother? Nothing? Everything?

She couldn't have saved his mother for him. Even if she'd called someone, there wouldn't have been enough time to save anyone. Why had Gina called her? They said the dying had partic-ular messages to communicate to particular people. What had Gina wanted to say to her? *Louise,* she'd said. She'd been dying, and Louise had listened, hung up, and lied about it. She had her reasons, she'd told herself a million times since.

She was crying.

Michael was next to her. He was patting her back like a toddler petting a dog.

"Ma? What's the matter? What happened?"

Steven was still in the street. Here, she wanted to say to Michael, bringing him to the window.

She wiped her eyes and ducked away. She closed the drapes and turned on a lamp.

"It's nothing," she said. "Thinking about your father."

It was what she said when she didn't want to pursue something. Michael didn't like him. He didn't mourn his absence, and didn't like to be reminded that his mother did.

"He's dead," he said.

"Yes, he is," she said.

Steven came back the next day and the day after that. Tuesday night, sleepless at 3 A.M., she went to her window and there he was on the stoop, smoking a cigarette, stuffing his hands in his pockets between drags.

She slipped on a pair of sweatpants under her nightgown, socks, slippers, a robe, and sneaked into Michael's room. He had the bedroom set he'd had as a boy. Two twin beds, a night table between them, a three-drawer dresser, a small desk and chair. A customer of Elia's had been upgrading for his own son and they'd gotten the whole set cheap.

He was on his back, his knees tenting the covers. He slept like an infant, his head turned to one side, his fists by his ears. He was grinding his teeth.

She pulled his chair over and sat next to the bed. Boxes of crackers, cookies, and cereal were lined up on his night table and desk. She used to insist he keep food in the kitchen. She'd given up on that years ago.

Behind the boxes were his stacks of school composition books. He never took them out of his room. He'd never said she couldn't, but she'd never looked in them, even after the murder. He had a certain kind of pen he liked using.

He stopped grinding, and his face relaxed. She stroked his forehead. He used to go months without a haircut, until a few years ago when it had grayed and thinned so much the barber on the corner had convinced him to get a buzz cut. It looked better this way.

She slid her hand under his and regarded him. Here was her boy.

On her way downstairs, there were still empty wine and vodka bottles scattered in front of Gina's old apartment. She would have to talk to Manuel again. A man, too old for college, stepped backward into the hallway. He pulled one of the girls after him, his hand against her cheek. "Beautiful you," he said. "Days aren't days without you." Over the girl's shoulder, he saw Louise watching. He was like a movie star caught off guard. He winked at her. Louise was embarrassed for him. She frowned and picked her way around the bottles to the stairs.

By the time she got outside, Steven was gone.

Something was happening.

First Michael had gone upstairs to Charlie's, and then he had come back, going straight to his room. Now someone was knocking on the front door.

It was four in the afternoon and Louise was in bed. She'd been there all day. No energy for anything else. Steven hadn't come, as far as she knew.

"Michael," she called. "The door."

She called some more. The knocking was still going strong.

She put on her robe and went to the door. It was Charlie's father. He'd been down to their place a couple of times, and even in his mailman uniform, his presence was disconcerting. A big black man on her threshold.

His name was TJ. He looked embarrassed. He had a rolled-up magazine in his hand.

"I already got my mail," she said.

"Listen," he said. "I don't wanna make a big deal outta this, but we just can't have him showing this kind of stuff to Charlie."

She could hear a door opening and closing up the stairs. Probably his wife eavesdropping. She never came down to do the talking.

"How do you know it's Michael's?" she said.

The year before, Michael had rented *Deep Throat* for Charlie. A few months ago they'd taken some of TJ's marijuana and smoked it in Charlie's room. Sometimes after they'd been around, she found wadded-up napkins in odd corners.

TJ handed the rolled-up magazine to her. "I'm sorry," he said. "I know he don't mean nothing."

Brenda, Charlie's mother, leaned over the banister one floor up. "He's ten, Louise. T-e-n. What's a grown man wanna hang out with a ten-year-old for anyway?"

TJ looked pained. "I got it covered, Bren," he said.

Louise hated her with her hennaed hair and her tattooed ankles. Her brown kid with that crazy hair. Her *mulignan* husband.

"She's just talking," TJ said.

Before Charlie there'd been a kid from down the block. Before that, from the park. Before that, Steven. Michael was a kid himself. He had a good heart, a big heart. Sometimes people didn't understand that.

"Maybe Charlie shouldn't come around for a while," she suggested before TJ could.

TJ looked relieved. "Yeah, sure. Good idea."

She closed and locked the door. The door to Michael's room was closed. She stood outside it for a minute. His music was playing.

Years ago she'd gone down to the basement to put in a load of laundry. Michael had been crying in the far corner of the laundry room, a glass jar held up to his face.

She put the magazine facedown in front of his door and went back to bed.

When she woke it was dark out, and Muriel was there in the rocker, beading a necklace. For the last few years, she'd made her own jewelry. Big wooden things with feathers and rope. She put the pile aside.

"Good morning," she said.

Pain, in her chest and her side. Her doctor had said the cancer would go from lungs to liver to bone to brain. She was supposed to call him for a morphine prescription when she needed to.

Her body was ingesting itself. Her brain would swell. There'd be a coma.

Muriel pulled the covers back. "Come on," she said. "Tea. In the living room. Everyone's invited."

Louise noticed Michael hovering in the doorway. He cocked his head and gave her a small wave.

Getting out of bed was harder than she expected. She felt like she'd spent the day lifting heavy objects. She imagined a giant crank handle inside of her spooling her up from the inside out. Muriel took her hand and elbow and lifted her to her feet. She helped her into her robe and said softly, "Time to come clean."

Muriel made tea. Even Michael had a cup. He hated tea. Louise told him to add more sugar. "Nah," he said. "I'm good."

"Michael called," Muriel said. "He was worried, wanted to know what was wrong. I told him I couldn't tell him, but I could come over here and make sure you did."

Michael looked into his teacup, as if trying not to overhear. He sneaked looks at his mother.

It broke her heart to look back at him.

She closed her eyes and covered her face with her hands.

Muriel put a hand on her knee. "Your mother has cancer, Michael," she said.

Louise couldn't bring herself to open her eyes. She listened for him.

"Yeah, so?" he said.

Muriel shook Louise's knee gently. "You're up," she said.

Whenever she opened her eyes now, it took seconds for her vision to clear. She and Elia used to take turns spinning Michael as a toddler around and around in Elia's barber chairs, and then they'd set him on the ground, all of them laughing as he tipped and stumbled.

She couldn't bring herself to say anything. She was getting one chance after another, and look how well she was doing.

"It's gonna be okay," she said.

Muriel exhaled. "Louise," she said. She turned toward Michael in her social worker pose. "It's not the kind of cancer anyone can fix," she said. "We need to tell you what to expect. We need to work out how you'll live after your mother's gone."

Michael put his cup down on the floor under his chair. He brought his shoulders up to his ears and then let them fall.

"Muriel," Louise said, hoping to get her out of the house with as little fuss as possible.

"Your mother's going to die," Muriel said. "And we need to talk about what that will mean for you."

He crossed the room and put a finger on her chest. He started with *liar* and *bitch* and kicked the coffee table over. Teacups and spoons skidded to the wall. Things broke. Muriel didn't panic. She'd seen his episodes before.

Louise put a hand on his arm, but he shook it off. "You don't talk to me," he said, pointing at her. His eyes were full of fear and rage and betrayal.

She stood up. He pushed her back down. "You think you're leaving?" he said.

She'd brought him into this world. She'd made him who he was, and now she *was* leaving. There wasn't anything to do to get rid of that kind of rage.

Even before the murder, she'd been telling herself that they made out okay, that they could take care of themselves. She could handle him. Who was she kidding? Neither of them had been okay in years. Michael may never have been okay.

One of the neighbors must've called the police. Maybe the unfriendly girls downstairs. By the time the two officers arrived, he was calmer. He was in his chair, hands under his thighs. Muriel let them in. Louise was on her hands and knees, piling broken china into a cupped hand.

Relationships were sorted out. The police asked their questions. The three of them gave their answers. Louise did not want to press charges and was not in any danger. Muriel agreed. The officers were persuaded.

One suggested Michael might want to take a walk around the block. Cancer, everyone agreed, was a tough one. One of the officers said his mother had beat it just last year, and that Louise shouldn't give up hope.

Michael got his jacket and went out in his slippers. Louise couldn't tell if anyone noticed.

The officers lingered. One of them carried the broken china into the kitchen and came back out with the dustpan and hand broom. The other righted the coffee table.

Here they are, Louise thought. Tell them what you know.

"He's not dangerous," Muriel said. "Just a little troubled."

"Who isn't?" one officer said, sweeping.

"You should meet my brother," said the other.

Everyone smiled, and the tension continued to drain from the room. Michael was odd. He was eccentric. He was a disappointment to his mother. He wasn't a murderer. Everything would be fine. They'd be okay. They always had.

The officers left. Louise watched from the window. Steven was back on his stoop, watching the cop car, and the cops. How long had he been there?

Her son was like a toy train she was trying to keep on its tiny rails. She was exhausted. It was exhausting.

Muriel was next to her. Louise put her head on her friend's shoulder. She didn't think Muriel would recognize Steven. Still, she said she needed to sit, and led her back to the sofa.

"You need to get help," Muriel said.

Louise bent to pick up a teacup piece the officers had missed.

"For yourself, and for Michael," she said.

Louise didn't say anything. It was her special talent.

"I'll call the doctor tomorrow," she said. Deflection, distraction: other things she was good at.

Muriel left, and Steven was still there. Michael came home and passed her without a word, closing the door to his room firmly if not loudly. Steven was still there. She almost expected to see his mother sitting next to him. They'd both been gone for years, but in another way they'd both been there all this time, waiting for her to come out and play.

Michael didn't come out of his room for two days. He dragged the tiny kitchen TV in there. He had his music. He had his cereal boxes. She came home from the store or the laundry and found evidence that he'd emerged. A bowl of picked over grapes on the coffee table or an unwrapped packet of cold cuts on the counter. At night in bed, she heard him moving around the apartment.

The first night, she went out to the living room and he wasn't able to look at her. He just sat there. When she asked if she could sit with him, he didn't say yes.

Steven was on his stoop both nights. She found herself thinking that God was offering some kind of deal, but she couldn't figure out what it was. Who did she think she was, making deals with God?

Muriel got tired of Louise putting her off, and hand-delivered her to the doctor. He filled a prescription for morphine, writing out the dosages in block print. He reminded her about hospice, about social workers. She nodded, even wrote things down.

The morphine gave her headaches, made her feel like she was moving when she wasn't. Even though Michael wasn't talking to her, she worried that a mother on morphine made him nervous. She took three doses and then stopped. The symptoms of cancer or the side effects of drugs: what difference did it make? Everything was a version of pain.

She called from the pay phone at the coffee shop on 112th and talked to Miss Samantha Cook and told her what she knew. Her dime ran out. She fished out another and called back. Louise was plain and clear. She tried to sound rational and intelligent. She tried not to cry when asked why she'd waited so long. She could hear the woman taking notes on the other end. Things to check. Muriel had said she had to let the professionals do their jobs. This wasn't what Muriel had meant, but it seemed to Louise that the principle applied. She described what she'd seen. What she thought it might've meant stretched between herself and the young woman like a rope with any number of uses.

The trial was a week away. Miss Cook wanted to meet with Michael.

Louise faltered for the first time during the conversation. She hadn't imagined that, though she understood it was stupid that she hadn't. What had she thought? They'd hear her out, let Benjamin Engel go, and never bother any of them again?

She agreed to bring him to the office the next day at three. She replaced the handset, opened the booth door, and sank to her rear end. Maybe she was dying right here, right now. Why not? It made perfect sense. When had she been more ashamed?

thirteen

the frightened waitress had called the ambulance. The para-
medics had taken her to Columbia Presbyterian. The emergency
room doctor had admitted her. Things were happening. The
phone call had made her life less her own.

Muriel was there. Michael wasn't. She was going to die without family.

"Where's Michael?" she said.

Muriel came to the edge of the bed. The top of Louise's hand
was sore. There were tubes and bandages. Machines making their
noises. The whole thing seemed like too much fuss.

"He's home," she said. She saw Louise's face and added, "He did
the right thing. He said to call when we knew something."

"What is there to know?" Louise asked, closing her eyes again.

Her friend didn't answer. The woman on the other side of the
curtain was moaning softly. Louise nodded in her direction. "How
long has that been going on?"

"She doesn't know she's doing it," Muriel said. "She's pretty
out of it."

"That's better?" Louise said. She sat up. She hunted around in the sheets for the nurse's bell.

Louise had never seen Muriel at a loss. "I must be in bad shape," Louise said.

Muriel tried unsuccessfully to change her expression. Louise was moved by the attempt.

The nurse arrived, a young woman with dark red hair pulled back into a ponytail.

"I need to get outta here," Louise said. "Be a good girl and get my clothes."

The nurse and Muriel exchanged looks.

"You're where you need to be," Muriel said. The nurse nodded, glad to have someone who seemed to know what she was doing on her side.

"I'm dying," Louise said. "I don't have to die here." She struggled with the bars on the side of her bed, then gave up and tried to swing her legs over them. A foot got stuck. The hospital gown twisted.

She turned her eyes on Muriel, her best and only friend. "Help me," she said. And then she was crying, for what she had done and for what she knew about herself. Had she brought this down on herself, or had it been handed to her? And this death coming for her: whose responsibility was that?

They wouldn't let her leave until they were satisfied that the situation at home was adequate to meet her needs. Louise asked Muriel what they cared about what her needs were. What did they care where she died? Muriel told her to humor them, which made Louise know her friend was humoring *her*.

And so, hospice. Less than a month after the young doctor had given her the news, her own bed pushed aside to make room for a hospital one. IV stand, oxygen, monitors. A nurse qualified to give sponge baths and dole out morphine lined up to come and go a few hours a day. Referrals for specialists in emotional support and pamphlets about family groups, other people in the same little boat of misery. All of it paid for by insurance.

Gerli, the—Filipino? Singaporean?—nurse was smaller than Louise, but lifted her from wheelchair to bed with an ease that made Louise nervous. She made competent Muriel seem irrelevant.

Michael hadn't come out of his room. Muriel had knocked as they'd passed, saying it was only them, but he hadn't responded, his music playing softly behind the closed door.

She'd been in the hospital for four days. Had he been in his room the whole time? The house smelled different. As if he'd been eating out of cans for four days. He probably had.

Muriel told her that neighbors had been filling their freezer and fridge with ready-to-go dinners. Even the unfriendly girls downstairs. The thought of other people feeding Michael made her dizzy with grief.

Had Miss Cook tried to get in touch with her? Had she talked to Michael? She sent Muriel away, thanking her, telling her to come back later, promising her she would rest.

She lay in her at-home hospital bed, Gerli taping tubes here and there around her. What kind of woman gave herself to the dying? Louise guessed she should admire the behavior, but she didn't. It angered her.

Today was Thursday. The trial began on Monday. She hadn't

given the lawyer her phone number, but she had given her name. Had she called? Had she talked to Michael?

"I need the phone," she said to Gerli.

Gerli stared at her. She didn't speak English all that well. Louise wondered how much she'd understood. "Phone," Louise said, making dialing motions with her finger, holding a fist to her ear.

"I understand," the tiny woman said. "No phone." She pointed to the pillow beneath Louise's head. "You sleep."

And as if she were some kind of fairy or witch, Louise did.

When she woke, it was dark. The room was hot. Apparently Gerli believed in heat. And humidity. There were two metal pans filled with water steaming and hissing at either end of the heater. Louise recognized them from her kitchen.

She felt worse than when she'd gone to sleep. Drugged, thick. Her eyes were sore.

Michael was there.

Seeing him made her happy.

"How ya doing?" she asked.

"Okay," he said.

He was wearing the same clothes he'd had on the last time she'd seen him, and holding that plastic puzzle cube she'd given him the last time she'd gone to the hospital, for her gallstones. He liked puzzles.

"You want to talk?" she said.

"Not really," he said. He wasn't being rude.

She tried to guess what time it was. Late. Almost early. The sky was that blue.

"Steven's been coming around," he said.

The thickness in her head cleared. "Yeah, I saw him," she said. Like they were talking about the mailman or the plumber. "You talked?" she asked.

He nodded.

"What did he say?" she asked.

He shrugged and she recognized her own gesture. What had she given him? What would she leave him with?

"He lives in New Mexico," he said. "He works in a mountain bike shop."

"New Mexico," she repeated.

"He liked bikes," he said. "He seemed okay," he added.

Her head was foggy again. She wasn't sure what this conversation was about.

"He said he had been wrong," Michael said.

"About what?" she asked.

"He said the worst thing wasn't that his mom was gone."

Michael must not have heard right. Of course that was the worst thing.

"He said the worst thing was that he never *knew* anything."

Michael seemed uninterested in what she thought of the comment, but just like that, Steven went from being an image of Michael to being an image of herself.

"Could you open the window?" she asked.

A channel of cold air worked its way through the room.

"His dad's lawyer's looking for you, he said. He said you called her." Michael's face was like none of this had anything to do with him.

She thought about lying. After all this, she thought about lying to her only son. *Amazing* was one word for it.

So she told him the truth. She told him about the phone call from Gina. How, if she was being really really honest, she had to admit that she'd probably known who it was.

He frowned. "How could you know?" he said. "Those kind of sounds?"

"She said my name," she said.

He was quiet. Then he said, "Still."

He wasn't acting like someone talking about a murder he'd committed. He was trying to make her feel better. But she couldn't be sure. Why couldn't she be sure? Her heart was breaking.

"So why *didn't* you call anyone?" he asked.

"Telling the truth is hard," she said. It was the truth.

He nodded and raised his eyebrows like she'd said something remarkably smart.

"I told the lawyer," she said. "She wants to talk to you, go over what you know." In the midst of her self-hatred, she watched him for signs. Of what? What did she know about the signs a murderer gave out?

"Sure," he said.

Louise closed her eyes. She was on her deathbed manipulating her son. And she was worried about what *he'd* done?

Miss Cook came to the house on Friday. Outside, the sun was staggeringly bright. It was colder than it looked. Brown and red leaves fell from the trees.

She was wearing jeans and a turtleneck sweater, and some makeup. She looked too young to be a lawyer. Or too young to be any good. She was blonde and fit.

She said she'd grown up a few blocks away. She shook their

hands, even Gerli's. She told Louise she was sorry about her illness. She included Gerli in the small talk. She was kind to Michael in a matter-of-fact way, and Louise felt judged and chastised. She said to call her Sam.

She suggested that she and Michael talk in the living room. Let Louise get some rest.

Once, Louise heard laughing. "What are they doing?" she said to Gerli.

Gerli looked up from her magazine. "Talking?" she offered.

Louise realized that she had no idea what would happen next. The girl called Sam could go away and never come back or lead Michael away in handcuffs.

She appeared at the door alone. Michael was in his room, she said. She was holding a yellow pad.

"Thank you," she said. "For calling." She said that Benjamin wanted her to express his gratitude.

Louise had heard that the inmates at Rikers Island could hear the jets taking off and landing right over them.

"You did the right thing," Sam said.

"What did he say?" Louise asked, her heart lurching and rocking in its little cage.

Sam shook her head a little. She would check things out, talk to her partners. She'd be in touch.

The whole thing had taken less than an hour.

That night Michael sat with her. Across the small room, in the armchair that had been Elia's mother's, he sat with his hands over his knees.

She had a low fever. Her vision went from clear to cloudy with what started to seem like the regularity of breaking waves. Gerli seemed unsurprised. She pointed at Louise's head. "Brain," she said. "Little bit swelling."

"It's okay," she said before leaving for the night, and in the strangeness of the night, they believed her.

Outside, it was raining. No thunder or lightning, just heavy, heavy rain, coming straight down. The trees darkened and bowed, the last of their leaves falling wetly to the ground. The sky went from washed-out green to cloudy gray, and then something darker. Louise had no idea what time it was.

Sometimes he talked, sometimes he didn't. Sometimes she heard and understood him, sometimes she didn't, her mind lost in the predictable wanderings of morphine, illness, and age. She chose not to bore him with the details. Elia had always wanted to tell her his dreams. In a man otherwise so reticent, she'd found it an unappealing habit. She was glad that his early death had spared her his aging.

"What did you tell Sam?" she asked.

He tilted his head—an odd and giant bird. "What do you think I told her?"

"What you knew?" she suggested.

"What I knew," he said.

There wasn't anything in his voice.

Go ahead, it said. Ask me what you want to know.

"Did you kill her?" she asked.

Her eyes were closed, and there was silence from him for so long that she thought she might not have spoken out loud. The rain made its metallic noises against the fire escape. Water poured through the drainage pipe loud as a waterfall. There was the smell of wet earth and waste. Up above, past the birds and monkeys on their high perches, the snakes coiled around limbs like thick, brilliant bracelets around native arms, the swarms of insects veering their way between branch, leaf, and flower. Past all that, a small patch of sky, white and flat, too bright to look at.

Michael was next to her. She opened her eyes. The sadness on his face was like pain.

"You think I did," he said.

Answer him, she thought.

She reached out and held his finger with her hand. He pulled away and wiped at his face.

"I'm sorry I've been such a mess," he said, stepping away from the bed.

She'd never heard him sadder. His face was a vast field of defeat.

"I gotta go," he said. His voice sounded like it did sometimes, an animal pacing a cage.

"Oh, stay," she said, her voice full of longing.

He shook his head sadly. "I gotta go," he said again, as if it were all the vocabulary he could manage.

Sit up, she thought, her eyes closed, trying harder. Get out of this bed and tell him what he's been for you.

She said his name. She opened her eyes. She was alone.

In the morning, he was gone.

He hadn't left a note, but Gerli was holding the coffee can from the kitchen where the fifty dollars used to be. "We call someone," she kept saying, and Louise kept agreeing, though neither of them moved for the phone.

A fist closed around her heart. What had she done? What had

she brought upon herself? This and other moments that were coming. And when it was her turn to leave this world she'd be like Gina: She'd know who she wanted to talk to and what she wanted to say. And he wouldn't be there.

His whole life he'd been waiting for her to show him that he was damaged, that he inspired nothing but shame. And now she had. She didn't care what happened to Benjamin Engel. She didn't care what Michael had done. That was the truth. He wouldn't be there. Now or later. She would die without him.

"You want see his room?" Gerli asked.

She shook her head. His room would look the way it had always looked.

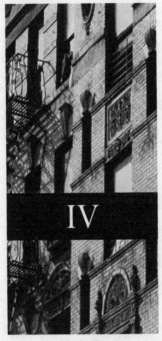

Memorial Day 1972

fourteen

the weather was cooperating. The picnic blankets and lawn chairs were spread and set on dry ground not yet covered by summer ants. The sun was warm. The breeze was light. The clouds were big and white. Memorial Day: everyone enjoying a reprieve from their regular lives. Nothing unusual about it, but still, they felt blessed. Or at the very least, lucky.

The block association was new, the idea of a few longtime residents nervous about the decline of the neighborhood and the decreasing effectiveness of the police. If they didn't solve a murder in seventy-two hours, it was likely never to be solved. Every week, more muggings. A few months ago, a string of burglaries, never solved. Muriel Yablonsky, from 326, had woken up to find a man in a knit hat standing over her. Last month a man shot and killed as he ran down the center of the street. Larry Abrams, from 345, had held the man's head in his lap.

Bars were going up on windows and extra locks on doors. Advertising flyers for alarm companies were appearing in mailboxes, but no one had the money to afford them.

The more conservative of the longtime residents voted Democratic. Most of them were Socialist. They believed in the mix of classes. They were divorced mothers, interracial couples, artists, and teachers instead of lawyers and insurance agents. They understood that their values were not genetic, that they could make their own way. They admired get-up-and-go, spunk, and minding their own business. They cared about each other, at least in theory. Theirs was a community of people who were living lives different from the ones that had been expected of them. They were trailblazers or misfits, depending on your angle of vision.

This was the first purely social gathering of the group. A picnic in Riverside Park. Potluck. There'd been sign-up sheets posted in lobbies. They'd begun making their way down the hill to the park at midday, an odd parade, bearing their plastic containers.

Steven had not wanted to come. He was eight and didn't like crowds. The kinds of questions grown-ups tended to ask left him confused and sullen. He *looked* sweet. It bothered people that he wasn't.

He sat on a rock on the fringes of the party and eyed his mother. He didn't like her at parties. They didn't go to many. She was a nurse with long hours. She didn't have a husband. He didn't have a father.

Last week in the middle of the night, his mother had woken him. She was already wearing her coat, and put his on over his pajamas and carried him to the elevator, which he liked. She almost never carried him anymore. He was too heavy, she said. How did she get such a big boy?

She carried him to Riverside Drive and turned the corner. It was cold and the air felt wet, as if somewhere nearby a sprinkler was on. The parts of his body on hers were warm. The other parts weren't. He missed his bed. She'd forgotten his slippers.

She put him in the backseat of a parked car with the engine still running and the windows open. A man was in it smoking a cigarette. The radio was on low. Baseball.

She sat in the front. The man handed her a cigarette and lit it for her. He didn't look back at Steven. Steven decided not to look at him either. His mother's hand was posed out the open window. The smoke curled up into the light from the streetlight and disappeared. He liked it. He didn't know why he liked things like that.

She'd never brought him into a car before. Her friends usually came to the apartment after she thought he was asleep. They'd talk in low voices. Sometimes he recognized the voices; sometimes he didn't. The sounds of the conversations made him nervous, and he fell asleep almost immediately. It was what he did when he was nervous.

He didn't know what to do in a car. He sat in the backseat with a blanket around him, his thumb in his mouth. She'd told him he had to stop sucking his thumb. He didn't see what it had to do with her. He would suck his thumb his whole life.

She had photographs of some of the men on the wall in their hallway. Her girlfriends thought it was weird. None of them were of this guy.

They still weren't talking. His mother seemed to be waiting for something. It made *him* more hopeful.

The other day at school, the class had been lined up at the door, on the way to music, and he'd bent down to tie his shoelace. Trying to hurry, to not hold up the line and call attention to himself, he'd had a clear, loud thought. He'd get bigger. His looks might change a little. But everything else was already the way it was going to be.

He didn't want to be like his mother, but he didn't know who else to be like.

Lily waited until one to make the walk down to the park. She was carrying almond junket in a glass bowl. Why did she do things like this to herself? Why did she say yes to things like this, knowing what they'd be like before they even started? And then why did she always do something to make herself stand out even more?

She entered the park and headed down the hill. She fell in step with a well-dressed guy about her age. He was blond, one of those prep-school boys. He was pushing a kid's bike, no kid in sight.

He smiled at her. "Whadja get for me?" he asked. He was the kind of good-looking that made her blink.

Attention like this didn't often come her way. "I'm meeting people," she said.

He seemed to have lost interest. He gave her words a wave. A silver bracelet with an infinity sign slipped down his forearm. He veered off to the right.

There were Muriel Yablonsky and Luis, their super. She didn't know anyone else, having lived here less than a year. She wondered how long it would take for someone to comment on her looks.

And what are you, dear? Vietnamese?

So why had she brought almond junket, the one dessert she could be absolutely certain no one would ever have heard of or seen?

Oh, how *interesting*. Is it a family recipe?

And, of course, then the inevitable mortification of having to say that it was. The only specialty of her parents that she'd learned how to cook. Whenever a dish was required of her, she made this. What was wrong with her?

Muriel spied her and beckoned her over. Muriel's husband was not there. He seemed to be around less and less these days. Meanwhile, Muriel grew more and more formidable. She strode toward Lily like the Statue of Liberty had pulled free of her moorings.

"Lily Chin," she said loudly, as if in terms of an introduction that was all that was necessary, and then embraced her in a large Jewish wingspan. Lily felt like one of the urchins beneath the robes of the Ghost of Christmas Present.

"Hello," she said. She held out the junket. "This is from my mother. A family recipe."

Muriel was thrilled. She called people over. "It's Oriental," she said, pulling back the foil cover.

People stared at Muriel's friend, kindly.

"Isn't she lovely," Muriel said. "She's a graduate student." She paused. "At Teacher's College."

There were appreciative sounds all around.

An older woman put a hand on Lily's head. "Look at this hair," she said. "Och. What I wouldn't give."

Lily stood there. She was the only Asian here, and she wasn't a member of the block association, though Muriel, who was, had stopped her outside their building to give her a whistle and an air horn and to show her how to use them in case she happened to spy anything suspicious.

Their job, Muriel had said, was to get the police there as quickly as possible. They were not to take the law into their own hands, she'd added, as if this were something she knew Lily was desperate to do.

"I can't stay long," Lily had answered, glancing back up the street she had just come down.

Now Muriel led her toward the tables and chairs, the food and drink. She leaned in. "There are eligible men here," she said.

Lily squinted at them. A man in his forties stood off to the side under a tree. He looked like the kind of man in whom she might inspire flashbacks. Some of the handymen and supers from the block stood in a little clump looking awkward out of their uniforms. An old man in a wheelchair wore a yarmulke.

Farther toward the river, away from the party, a couple with their young daughter had a picnic of their own. Lily recognized the father from the school where she'd had an internship that spring. To the left, a group of Hare Krishnas chanting and ringing their bells. Farther on, a boy on a rock.

They walked to the building where Michael worked as a night watchman. Michael let him work the elevator.

Steven tried not to show his excitement. Michael showed him how to pull out the handle and then push it left for down, right for up.

"What floor?" Steven asked.

"Basement," Michael said.

Past the laundry room was a thin door with NIGHT WATCHMAN painted on it in black letters.

It was a small room, as big as Steven's bathroom. There was a short padded bench in one corner, different-sized hand weights under it. A punching bag. An old door on top of two filing cabinets. On the door were model airplanes, some finished, some not. Their boxes were set up carefully against the wall. He could smell the glue. Under the table, a tiny fridge made a low hum.

It smelled nice. Like wood that had just been sawed in half.

"Cool, right?" Michael asked.

Steven liked the tiny fridge the best.

"Can I use that?" he asked, pointing at the punching bag.

"Sure, sure," Michael said. Sometimes, when he talked, he closed his eyes.

Steven was embarrassed at first and pushed at the bag with an open hand. It was heavier than he'd expected. He liked the feel of it. His mother had a bag made out of the same stuff.

Michael came around and stood behind the bag, leaning into it with his shoulder. He showed Steven how to punch it. It felt good. Like how he felt when he really pretend-drummed to his mother's favorite songs.

It was hot. The wood smell was from packets of cedar chips that were hanging from the pipes on the ceiling.

Michael reached around and put his hand to Steven's armpit. Steven jumped. "Tickles," he said.

Michael put his fingers in his mouth.

Steven stared. "I'm gonna go," he said. He couldn't remember what street they were on, which way they'd walked to get here.

"You sure?" Michael said. He seemed disappointed. His fingers were still up by his nose.

"I'm gonna go," Steven said.

"Okay," Michael said. "Come back another day. Anytime you want."

"See ya," Steven said, stopping at the door.

Michael was bent over a model. His back was to him. He didn't say anything.

Steven hoped he wasn't mad. "Okay?" he said.

Michael turned around and smiled. "Okay," he said.

Louise sat in the folding chair, her face to the sun. She loved the sun. Everything was better in the sun.

She'd seen a nature special on African Bushmen, trackers in the desert. Tiny, delicate men the color of polished wood, no taller than boys, reading the clues of the desert. The show had said they knew that the lizard was behind the rock. They didn't have to see it. Louise had found the whole thing extremely appealing.

She turned her head toward the tree Michael had been leaning against. She thought it a minor triumph that she'd gotten him to come at all, and tried not to let it bother her that he wouldn't actually join the group.

She scanned the edge of the park behind her. He was heading up Riverside Drive with Steven. They were holding hands.

Gina was in her it's-a-party-so-I'm-having-fun mode. She'd been drinking from the pitcher of vodka and lemonade she'd brought. She'd taken off her shoes hours ago. Steven was not on her mind. Louise decided to keep it that way. Gina had been dealt a tough hand. Let her relax. Let the boys have their fun too, she thought. It was a nice day. Let everyone have their fun.

lily should've left earlier. That woman who was demanding so much of everyone's attention, whom Lily had found unappealing to begin with, was just getting worse and worse. And now her son was missing.

She didn't even know the woman's name. She didn't want to be part of a search party. She didn't want to be part of anything.

The woman was drunk but determined to appear efficient. Lily was embarrassed for her. She wondered if it would be possible to slip away unnoticed. It was, after all, something she was good at, even known for.

The woman hadn't even noticed her son was gone until everyone started to pack up. The thing had gone on for hours. Goodwill had turned to impatience. The thought of cooking dinner was making people nauseous. There were still hours ahead of them before sleep.

Plastic cups with leftover soda, juice, vodka were emptied onto the grass. Someone shook out a garbage bag and held it open.

Her son seemed to be the last thing the woman thought of, but once she had, she seemed to know she had to pull herself together, and seemed even more aware that she was incapable of doing so. One of Lily's few friends in college had been the same way. "I'm a fuckup," she'd say over and over, doing nothing to change her ways. Lily had patience with people like that. Until she didn't.

The woman grabbed at Lily's arm and wanted to know when Lily had seen her son last.

Lily didn't know who he was. "I'm sorry," she said, passing her off to someone who knew her better.

Someone went to check the woman's apartment. Someone else ran up to the corner store.

Lily kept tidying up. She folded the blankets into small, neat squares and piled them up. When her mother had first moved to the States, she'd used tight stacks of blankets, sheets, and towels as furniture.

She gathered napkins that had sidled away. A plastic fork speared into the ground.

More people got involved. The woman seemed to lose what little useful energy she'd mustered. She sat on the grass holding her ankles.

The teacher that Lily had recognized came over carrying a pair of slip-ons, and asked the woman, "Are these yours?"

Lily could see that the woman was the kind of woman who attracted behavior of this kind. But she took a breath and tried not to be unkind. What did she know about men and women and the behavior between them? The teacher's patience felt like a rebuke. Maybe this woman was doing her best. Who was Lily to judge?

Steven had thought he knew which way the park was, but he'd walked for three blocks and then turned around and walked back the way he'd come. He sat on a stoop near a busy corner. Busy was safer, his mom said. If you looked like a chump, the world would treat you like a chump. He tried not to look like a chump.

A guy said, "Hey."

The guy looked up and down the block. He was pushing a kid's bike. He was wearing jeans and a dressy shirt. The sleeves were rolled up. He was tan. His hands looked like the kind of hands that could make things.

"Where's your mom?" the guy asked.

"In the park," Steven said. He looked at the bike. "That yours?" he asked.

The guy laughed. The sun was behind the buildings.

"I found it," the guy said. "I figured someone could use it. Like it?"

Steven got hot. He shook his head. "No, thank you." He didn't know how to ride a bike. "Nice sneakers," he said. They were green and white Adidas with gold lettering.

The guy looked down and rocked back on his heels. "Days aren't days without them," he said.

"Mine are Converse," Steven said.

The guy gave a low whistle. "Nice," he said.

Steven thought maybe he was making fun of him.

"Are you okay on your own?" the guy asked.

"Not really," Steven said.

The guy nodded as if agreeing with something wise. "I'm Matthew," he said.

"Okay," Steven said.

"So how about we find your mother?" he said.

His mother had told him about strangers, but he was going to find his mom anyway. He stood up and they started walking, the bike between them.

Everyone was still there. The sun was low over the river. It was hard for him to make out who was who in the group. Someone spotted them, pointed, and shouted. His mother broke free and came running toward them. It was like TV.

She dropped to her knees and hugged him, saying things. He was embarrassed, but glad to be there, and he put his arms around her, his cheek knocking into her shoulder.

He introduced her to the guy. She was grateful and nice. Matthew looked at her. Everyone stayed out a little longer. It was a celebration. It got dark, and still they stayed. Matthew promised to teach him how to ride a bike, and Steven knew he really would.

His mother said, "Let's raise a glass." She didn't have one, but said it anyway. She raised a hand.

He looked around. They were all there: people he knew and people he didn't. They'd been worried, and now they weren't. He'd been scared, and now he wasn't. It could happen that easily. Everything wasn't already the way it was going to be. Things could happen. Things could change. It was a good thing to know.

ACKNOWLEDGMENTS

Special thanks to Detective Larry Adams, Trudy Ames, Ellen Biben, Jason Clark, Cassandra Cleghorn, Sean Griffin, Sandra Leong, Robert McGuire, Dr. Paul Rosenthal, Marsha Recknagel, Geoff Sanborn, Eric Simonoff, Harold Takooshian, Sarah Towers, Claire Wachtel, and Gary Zebrun.

And to my husband, Jim Shepard, and our children, Aidan, Emmett, and Lucy.